the Sidekicks

Will Kostakis

HARLEQUIN® TEEN

ISBN-13: 978-0-373-21262-0

The Sidekicks

First published in Australia by Penguin Random House Australia

Copyright © 2016 by Will Kostakis

U.S. edition copyright © 2017 by Will Kostakis

www.HarlequinTEEN.com

Printed in U.S.A.

To all the teachers:

Rosalind McKenzie, for her guidance;
Peter Hipwell, for his advice;
Geoffrey Wren, for his point of view;
Samantha Kosky, for all her talk of rubber bands;
and Greg Bell, for looking at this first.

THE SWIMMER

"OH, WE ARE NOT ACTUALLY FRIENDS."

I have to give Miles credit. It takes real skill to be that insensitive. I mean, he's not wrong. When we hang out, people see a group of four, but really, we're three guys with the same best friend. The only thing Miles, Harley and I have ever had in common is Isaac. But when we're in the deputy's office and she's saying that something's happened to Isaac, that we should rely on each other for support, he could stand to be a little less right.

Harley groans. He has this general limpness to him, like a puppet missing half its strings. He sinks deeper into his chair. "Are you that thick?"

"I am not thick," Miles says.

That's true, he's not. He's second in our class. He's just never been very good with things that can't be measured in an end-of-year exam. Like the full spectrum of human emotion.

"I dunno, you're pretty ducking stupid."

"Harley, they know what you mean by *duck*." Miles turns to the deputy. "Right? You know."

I don't envy Kathy—*Mrs. Evans*. This would be hard enough if we got along, even slightly.

"Boys, this is a delicate situation. I am certain you are feeling many complicated emotions, but it's not productive to lash out at one another." She's being careful. She's speaking slowly and it's making her British accent more pronounced.

Miles scrunches his face. "Oh, we are not—"

Harley takes over. "This isn't lashing out. I'd say this is…40 percent?"

Miles corrects him. "Closer to 43."

"Cuz there's a *difference*."

"Well, it is a measure, so, yes, 40 and 43 are different."

"All right," Harley practically whispers. He turns to the deputy. "This is us at *43* percent animosity."

Mrs. Evans blinks. A pigeon flies past the window behind her. "Well," she continues eventually, "I think that it would be best if we—"

I interrupt her. "How did he die?" I ask.

Miles and Harley turn to me. They'd probably forgotten I was sitting between them. Mrs. Evans's office isn't that big; she's crammed three chairs in front of her desk in a space that fits only two. Our knees are touching, but when Miles and Harley have one of their little tiffs, it's amazing what they can't see.

"You said Isaac had an accident." I clear my throat. "What happened?"

Mrs. Evans takes a slow, deliberate breath. A moment to perfect her phrasing. "To be honest, Ryan, we don't know much. We know…generally."

Harley straightens up. "Then tell us generally."

"I would prefer to save that for when we speak to the entire junior class. We've organized for everyone to come to the chapel for the final half of fourth period." She checks her watch. "We have some time before then, so—"

"But you are sure?" Miles asks.

It takes Mrs. Evans a second to realize what he means. "Yes, Miles, we're sure."

He's the first one to cry.

———

Everything at Barton House is done in the Marist tradition, which is like regular Catholicism, only with a pinch of French. In the chapel, elaborate stained-glass windows depict *le chemin de croix*, lit from behind by lighthouse bulbs to give the illusion of God's love shining down from the heavens. In reality, the chapel is sandwiched between a storage room and the nurse's office.

This one time, a bulb burned out during a service, and Isaac shouted, "Who sinned?"

He cut through bullshit like that, and I can't believe he's…

Miles believes it. He's wiping his eyes on his sleeve. Harley's harder to read. He bites his right thumbnail.

We stand by the exit of the chapel. While the other

teachers herd their classes into pews, Mr. Collins comes over. He asks us how we are. We're silent.

From the back, we can see everything. Guys continue their conversations. They crack jokes. They check their phones. They have no idea why they've been pulled out of class. I want that back, the ignorance.

The bit before.

Mrs. Evans does most of the talking. I watch her words crash against the class. Two hundred individual reactions play out at once, intensifying at different speeds. For some, it's a slow burn; for others, an explosion.

Marty Johnson turns in his seat. He's probably said five words to me since laughing at a joke I made in seventh grade, but now he's staring right at me.

Others follow his lead. Suddenly, us standing in the back makes more sense to them.

And I start to feel it. Belief. Isaac is dead.

I need to get out. Mr. Collins understands. He helps with the door. (It's ridiculous how heavy that thing is.) When I'm certain it's shut, I squat a little, place my hands above my knees and face the floor. I take a deep breath. This helps with nerves, and apparently, having a friend die feels a lot like nerves.

Which makes no sense.

Which makes some sense.

Everything is different now. Course I'm scared shitless of that.

The more I focus on breathing, the less I think.

Inhale.

Exhale.

Someone struggles with the chapel door from the inside and I have the time to unfold myself and start pacing. Looks less wussy.

Mr. Collins wants to know if I'm all right. It's his job. I force a smile. "Yeah, I won't be long."

I'm not going back in. I imagine Mrs. Evans is seconds away from handing the reins to Mr. Ford, school counselor extraordinaire, or worse, to Brother Mitchell. I'm not really big on lighthouse love.

Mr. Collins disappears and Miles slips out before the door shuts. He didn't last much longer than me. I shouldn't stare but I do. He seems more panicked than upset. He keeps his distance, one hand on his side, the other on his forehead. His lips are moving, but I can't hear what he's muttering.

It's just the two of us. I should say something.

"You all right, man?"

He turns to me. His eyes are bloodshot. He doesn't reply.

"It's rough, isn't it?"

"Yes." Something occurs to him. Miles has difficulty censoring his face, so when something's going on in his head, it's pretty obvious. He takes a few hesitant steps toward me. "Do you happen to know Isaac's locker combination, by any chance?"

I shake my head. I can tell he's disappointed, but at the same time, he's relieved. Isaac didn't trust me more.

He mulls something over. I've always wondered what it's like inside Miles's head, thoughts processed and discarded before they'd even occur to anyone else our age.

Like the hulking all-terrain vehicles moms use for drop-offs, he's made for more than high school.

He straightens up. "Right. Tell Mr. Collins I have gone to the bathroom."

He starts down the hall in the wrong direction. Even for Miles it's weird. I jog to catch up.

"Where are you going?" I ask.

"The bathroom."

It's like a game of rock paper scissors. Grief trumps ignorance, but curiosity trumps grief. What's happening in the chapel seems so far away. I need to know what Miles is up to.

"You're not, though."

"I am breaking into Isaac's locker."

Oh. To be honest, I wasn't expecting him to tell the truth so soon.

"Seriously, go back and keep Mr. Collins busy."

"Why are we breaking into Isaac's locker?"

"Not *we*—*me*. I am doing it. You are going back to the chapel," he says.

"Why?"

Miles stops and sighs. I'm wasting his time and it's all over his face. "Isaac has something of mine and I want it back. Someone is going to open his locker at some point soon. I cannot let them find it."

That makes the curiosity worse. "What is it?"

He's growing impatient. "If you are going to follow me, you cannot ask that."

"But it's something bad?"

"I did not say that." He doesn't give me a chance to

ask another question before he adds, "We are going to need bolt-cutters. And a lock to replace the one we cut off so nobody suspects anything."

"There's a hardware shop near Martin Place. I could sprint."

"We have twenty minutes before the bell goes. It is not just a matter of you sprinting there—you would have to get past the ladies at reception, twice. I know there is one in Design and Tech, but that is locked up in the tool cage, so that leaves us with…"

It clicks for him first. When Mr. Collins isn't teaching economics, he looks after student stuff like class schedules and lockers. He has the bolt-cutters students use if they forget their lock combinations. And he's in the chapel at the moment, which means nobody's in his office.

"Come on." Miles launches himself into a door on our right. It swings open to the fire stairs. He climbs two steps at a time. This is a keenness to break school rules that I've never seen in him before.

What's in that damn locker?

I go to ask, but Miles escapes the stairwell and the door is closing. I leap over the last steps and catch it. Barton House occupies the first seven levels of a twelve-story building—wherever I need to be is usually three flights of stairs from wherever I actually am. This time we luck out—Mr. Collins's office is only one floor up.

Problem is, there's a four-foot-wide, floor-to-ceiling glass panel between his office and the hallway. Anyone walking past will notice the student who's broken in. And there's also the actual *breaking in* part.

I can feel the *he* job quickly becoming a *me* job. "Since you are here..." Miles begins. He tries to communicate the rest with a look.

"Me?" I ask.

"Your mom is a teacher."

"That doesn't mean I can just—"

He raises his hand to shut me up. "We do not have time."

"Oh."

"We need an alternative." He looks around. His eyes fall on the lone chair outside N4. He can't seriously be considering it.

"Yeah, let's not throw a chair through a glass panel," I say.

"I was not going to." He was totally going to. "But... how else are we going to get in?"

"Dude, no."

"Sorry, I have never broken into a teacher's office before."

"Well, neither have I." I grip the doorknob and twist. It turns. "Okay, now I have." I push the door open.

Miles stays put. "Go on, then," he urges.

Amazing what I'll do to satisfy curiosity.

I flick the switch and the light stutters to life. I scan the office for the bolt-cutters, but Mr. Collins doesn't leave them lying around in plain sight. I open desk drawers. Juice boxes, pens, manila folders—no bolt-cutters.

"Check under the desk," Miles suggests.

I watch him through the glass panel. "You're not coming in?"

He's stepped back a little farther for plausible deniability. "One of us needs to keep watch," he says.

Typical. I drop onto my stomach and start feeling around under the desk.

"You know what? I will fetch my lock and meet you at Isaac's locker," Miles says.

"Actually, I'd rather you stayed." I nudge Mr. Collins's sneakers aside and feel the space behind them. "Miles?" I worm forward a little and peer out the doorway. He's gone.

Great.

I worm back and continue searching. My hands close around a pair of handles.

Bingo. The bolt-cutters.

New thing I can say for certain: I look stupid with bolt-cutters stuffed under my shirt. I switch off the light and shut the door. Hoping no one leaves class early and notices my pointy boob, I hurry back down the hall, up the stairs and down an identical hall to Isaac's locker.

Miles is waiting, his lock hanging from his right index finger. We don't say anything at first, like locker 308 is something sacred. For a quiet second, grief defies the rules of rock paper scissors and trumps curiosity. There's a pang in my chest.

"All right, we do not have long," Miles says. "It is just a hole in the wall."

I pull the bolt-cutters out from under my shirt and line up the blades on either side of Isaac's lock. I squeeze the handles together until the blades meet. Miles reaches in and threads the broken lock out of the hole. He pockets the evidence and I open the door.

He swoops in before I can even get a look. He's knocking and lifting things, searching. I step back. Miles is a mess of frantic energy. What could have him so edgy?

A can of deodorant falls out and rolls to my feet. I pick it up. "Do you need any help?" I ask.

It's obvious he does. "No."

There's the sound of more knocking, lifting, searching.

"If you tell me what we're looking for, I can—"

"Where is it?" He runs his hands over where they've already been. "Where…is…it?"

He pushes away from the locker. It's the closest he's ever been to swearing. He walks around in a tight circle and looks like he's about to implode.

I try to calm him. "Look, nothing can be—"

"One thing," he says breathily. "I rely on him for *one* thing."

He crouches down, head resting on his fists.

I look to the locker. "Are you sure it's not here?"

"I am sure," he insists. "It is a red pouch. He must have taken it home. I told him never to take it home."

I step closer and put the deodorant back. At first glance, there's no red pouch, just some textbooks, loose paper and his sports bag. Instead of ransacking the locker like Miles, I go for the sports bag. Every so often, Isaac leaves his basketball stuff at school over the weekend to get out of Saturday sports. It's surprising how often that excuse flies. I open the bag and, yep, his unwashed gear from last week is in there. I gag. The smell is potently Isaac.

I stir the contents and catch a lick of red. I reach in and pull out a small zip pouch. I check over my shoulder. Miles is still crouched on the floor. Curious, I unzip. I see cash. Heaps of it. The pouch is filled with fifty-dollar bills.

"Um?"

Miles glances up and his eyes come alive. He's on his feet in an instant, snatching the pouch from my hands and zipping it shut.

"What?" I stammer. "How did you manage to—?"

"Just forget you saw that, all right?"

"Dude, that's like two grand, easy."

Miles shakes his head. He closes the door and threads the unbroken lock through the hole. He clicks it together and starts walking away.

"You're not going to say anything?"

Our eyes meet briefly. "This did not happen."

Five xylophone notes play over the school PA system. Whoever spearheaded the switch from a bell to percussion probably believed it was a gentler, less disruptive way to signal the end of class, but nope, we're an all-boys school. I can hear the catcalls and the chairs shifting.

Miles disappears down the fire stairs and I'm standing out in the open with—

Crap. Students explode into the hall. I tuck the bolt-cutters under my shirt. Looks pretty obvious, so I cross my arms. Still pretty obvious. Everyone's moving as one shouty mass toward the main stairwell. There's no way I can get into Mr. Collins's office, not without somebody noticing. He's probably on his way back from the chapel anyway. I need to hide the bolt-cutters somewhere more subtle.

I get to my locker. One arm folded over my chest, I manage to open the door. I plant the bolt-cutters behind my bag. A worry for later.

My lunch is up on the top shelf—a takeout container stuffed with chicken and brown rice. A quick zap in the junior common room microwave and it should be good to go. I reach for the container, then hesitate. I microwave my food, and what then? Eat at our usual spot? Stare at the space where Isaac used to be?

And… I'm not hungry anyway. I grab my swim gear instead. It's instinct. Once the guys from my grade get up here, I know there'll be a string of questions that I don't want to answer, that I don't know how to answer.

There's no one on duty in the aquatic center on Mondays.

I take the fire stairs down to the basement. It's deserted. The pool glows greenish blue in the dark. I leave the main lights off and cross the room. The water's persistent *csssh* drowns out the sound of my breathing.

Inhale.

Exhale.

I toss my bag on the floor, strip out of my uniform and slip on my Speedo. It's still wet from this morning, but it doesn't matter. I'll be soaked in a sec.

I step up onto the block and dive. The water folds over me, fingertips to toes. And the rest is habit, muscle memory, years of squad training echoing through my limbs. To the wall and back again.

I built my life in twenty-four seconds. I doze off in class and half-ass my homework, but so long as I train three hours a day and keep the blue ribbons coming, no one really cares. I'm on page five of the school brochure: Ryan Patrick Thomson, Olympic hopeful. I'm not full of myself, though. I pretend not to like it when people throw around words like *champion*.

We're a competitive squad. We're only as good as our last swim. When I stand on the starting block at every meet, I know I can lose it all before I reach the opposite wall. The starting gun fires, and I rebuild my life in twenty-four seconds. I swim fifty-meter freestyle, hit the wall, punch the air, and in return life's good to me. That's how it's always worked.

And we planned for it to keep working. Me on the Aussie team, a medal at the Games and a bad pun on the back page of the paper like *RY-NAMITE!* When we spoke about our futures, they were knotted. I'd get a sponsorship deal—multivitamins, probably. Isaac wanted more for me, though. He said I had a "selling watches" kind of face. "They pay the big bucks. You can afford to support my lifestyle then," he would joke but in a way that was also completely serious.

Tumble turn. Another lap. Another two.

Isaac aspired to the groupie life. And I didn't mind. Whatever I was given, I wanted to share with him. Like everything. He was the only person who *knew*, the only person I told. We didn't keep secrets. We didn't hide money for people without telling each other.

And what even was that? How does a guy like Miles

get hold of so much money? Working weekends? No, it's valuable study time. Besides, nobody hides their working-weekends money in a bag in someone else's locker. This is bigger than that, dirtier. And Isaac didn't just hide stuff; he got involved. Whatever went down, they were in on it together.

I collide with the wall. I grip the groove in the tiles with one hand and wipe the water off my face with the other.

"What were you up to, Isaac?" I whisper.

Csssh.

"People don't keep cash in bags." My eyes sting. I blink hard. "Were you guys in trouble?"

Csssh.

"And you can't just bail like this. We made plans." I'm not whispering anymore; it's a growl. It starts in my chest. Then I spit it out. "You're supposed to be *here*, so wherever you are, come back. This isn't over."

I blink into the almost-darkness. Nothing. Well, not nothing: *csssh.*

My face crumbles and I sob.

I'm talking to an empty room. The absence of a reply shouldn't upset me but it does. I can talk to Isaac as much as I like, but he's never going to talk back. Mrs. Evans tore a hole in my life this morning, and now that everything's still, I can finally see it. And it's getting bigger the longer I look at it.

The pendant lights hanging from the ceiling start to buzz and flicker. Someone's here. I inhale in bursts and submerge. From under the lane rope, I watch the unnatural white light intensify. Is a PE teacher doing the rounds? A group of kids using the pool during lunch? The last thing I want is an audience.

There's only so long I can stay underwater. I edge up against the wall and rise slowly. If I break the surface quietly and sneak a breath, I might be able to—

Mom's sitting on the starting block, carved from stone. "You can't be down here without a teacher."

"Like I'm gonna drown."

"There are rules."

"What's Kathy going to do? Expel me?"

"Mrs. Evans," she corrects. "And where are your goggles?"

"My eyes are fine."

I pull myself out of the pool and sit on the edge. I blow my nose between two fingers and flick it away. Mom's quiet. I look back at her and she smiles slightly.

Enough to remind me she's an army.

"You okay, kid?" she asks.

I shake my head.

———

Mom cancels my afternoon in the time it takes me to shower. No double Geography, no after-school laps, straight home. Driving out of the parking lot, Mom switches off the radio. It's as sure a sign as any that she's about to parent.

"So," she begins, "how are we going to play this?"

I'm leaning against the passenger window, feeling the vibrations of the car against my head.

"Would you rather we talk about it, or I distract you?"

"Distract," I croak. I clear my throat and try again. "Distract."

"Right." Mom taps the steering wheel as she conjures up a distraction. "Don refuses to admit he hit my car. I don't understand how. I have the security footage. He backs into the front, steps out of the car, inspects the damage, checks for witnesses, then drives away."

I can feel an ache spreading from my chest, so I focus on the distraction. "The school won't do anything?"

"It's not technically their parking lot or whatever—they won't go near it with a ten-foot pole. And then, insult to injury, I have to sit through assembly today and watch him win some Teacher of the fucking Year shit. He fucking hit my car. I want my money." Mom's expression sours. "Teacher of the Year. He probably nominated himself."

I wouldn't put that past him. Don is Mr. Butler, my Modern History teacher. That fact crosses Mom's mind. "I probably shouldn't be telling you this."

She's said that more times than I can remember.

She conjures a distraction from the distraction. "I was speaking to Beverly from St. Michael's this morning." Effortless segue. "There is big drama over there, trying to get the Model UN Conference off the ground."

The Model UN is Mom's extracurricular assignment. When the school hired her, she was given a choice between that and Chess Club, and well, one was slightly less sad than the other. Last year, Barton hosted the conference, and Mom was entrusted with making sure it went off without a hitch. Thanks to months (read: one late night the previous term with a bottle of red) of careful planning, it mostly did. *Mostly* because even carefully (read: drunkenly) planned conferences can unravel if people don't show up on the day.

On the morning of the conference, the teacher from Buckley's called to say the delegate for Italy had food poisoning. Mom needed an Italy for the day, or else calamity. I was her first choice. She pitched it as a day out of class. I resisted. Isaac said it was like the Sex Olympics for nerds. And what can I say? I was swayed.

"Are you doing it again this year?" she asks.

I shake my head.

"What was that, a shake or a nod? I'm driving." She glances my way, not long enough for me to repeat the movement, though.

"It was a no."

One hundred students sat at desks facing a podium, listening to each other's speeches. Some delegates dressed up—Japan came in a kimono and it was a bit much—but most of us were content in our uniforms. The other Barton kids wore their blazers; I wore my tracksuit. They sat up straight; my face collapsed into the palm of one hand. My eyelids drooped. I was slipping slowly into—

"Oi." Israel was holding out a folded piece of paper between two fingers. "Incoming diplomacy."

In neat cursive on the front: *To Italy.*

I unfolded the note.

The state of Norway hath noted your presence from across the room and requests that, should the appropriate opportunity present itself, Italy accompany Norway on an exploratory mission to the movies and perhaps share a large popcorn, if Italy is so inclined, it read.

The nations sat in alphabetical order. I turned around and the girl behind me smiled.

"Oh, don't act like it was so bad." Mom checks over her shoulder before changing lanes. "I'm sure it was *such* an imposition to miss out on class."

"I didn't really miss out," I say. "Mr. Rowland made me catch up on all the math."

"You just copied the answers out of the back anyway. And don't think Mr. Rowland never caught on."

"As if he did."

"I have lunch with these people every day, Ryan. We talk. You're seventeen, not subtle."

At the Model UN, the girl behind me smiled. I went to say hello when I noticed the tiny flag taped to the corner of her desk. Lebanon. Norway sat one row farther back. He was smirking. He.

I felt it like a spotlight. I'd been seen.

I snapped back to the front, hand trembling. I caught myself and pressed my fingertips into the desk. It was difficult to breathe, not that anyone would have noticed. I'm good at hiding. My face barely creased.

It was a nagging thought before it became a quiet certainty. And I had kept it secret and built the rest of me around it. I had expected Norway to be a she, expected to force a smile back, ask for her number, see a movie, kiss her, lose her number, boast about it. It would seem off if I didn't.

I can't remember not considering how people see me. I'm careful, always careful, maintaining a wall to hide behind, and he'd seen right through it.

Something had given me away. Sitting there, I combed over my recent past and tried to pinpoint the moment. Had there been a look that lingered too long? Had I said something? Could he just tell?

I was scared shitless. And something else. Underneath all that panic and fear, a faint, hopeful excitement scratched at my ribs.

The state of Norway hath noted your presence from across the room.

I was wanted. By someone I wanted to want back.

I was soaring, but still seated, and it felt like nothing else. And I wanted to turn and smile back and… Mom was hovering two rows ahead in full teacher mode and I plummeted. My world felt a little bit smaller.

"Besides," Mom adds after a sec, "I'm sure you made new friends last year."

I rest my head back on the glass. "Not really."

That's the thing about subtlety: do it well and no one notices.

I folded a note and wrote, *To Norway.*

His name was Todd, I found out. We saw a movie on a Sunday. I had never been so consciously aware of how close my body was to someone else's, but I kept to my side of the armrest and he kept to his. The credits rolled and I didn't want to leave. He didn't want to either, but when the cleaner tried to get at the popcorn under our seats, we got the hint. We bounced nervously off each other as we climbed the steps to the exit. I was halfway out the door when he grabbed my hand and pulled me back into the theater. The kiss was soft and explosive.

I didn't lose his number.

I pull my phone out of my pocket. Keeping it low, in the space between my seat and the passenger door, I check the screen. I have an unread message. Todd wants to know about my day. I say it's fine. His reply is instant. He's bored. It's the closest I've come to a normal conversation in hours. He asks what I'm up to. I can't lie. I tell him Mom's driving me home. He'll ask why I've left so early and I'll have to tell him.

I click back to the list of my latest conversations. My finger hovers over Isaac's name. I'm tempted to tap on it, revisit everything we've ever said. A new message from Todd stops me.

He asks why I've left so early.

———————

It takes us half an hour to get home. We've almost been here a year, but I can't get used to calling it that—home. It will always be my grandparents'. They built it in the early '90s with all the money they'd saved since moving here, and it was intended as a statement: "Started from the bottom, now look how high our ceilings are!" The tiled floors, the bulky intercom system in every room, the accents of black and gold, it all looked luxurious once. I grew up dreaming I'd have a house like it when I hit the big time, but now that we've inherited it, I miss our old place. Sure, it was cramped, and it smelled damp for days after it rained, but it was home. I had a space that was my own, and short of her bursting in with a megaphone, there was no way for Mom to broadcast announcements into it.

There's a *click*, the hum of background noise and then Mom's voice. *"Dinner's ready, Ryan."* Another *click*.

I glare at the intercom. A day doesn't go by without me fantasizing about ripping it off the wall and dismantling it.

I close my eyes, adjust myself and sink deeper into the mattress.

Click. "Now, darling." Click.

My plate is waiting on the kitchen counter. I hop onto the nearest stool. Mom insists she's not eating but she's overloaded my plate so she can pick from it whenever. I've barely made a dent before she reaches for the broccoli.

Mom leans back against the kitchen counter. "You can take tomorrow off," she says.

"I'm fine."

"It's not your call."

I cut hard into a piece of chicken breast.

"Seriously, I'm fine."

"I'm not fine, Ryan, so there's no way you are." Her voice wavers.

She doesn't get it.

Tomorrow I have Squad. Waking up will be a pain—

it always is. Mr. Watkins will write the sets of laps on the board—he always does. I'll swim them, because I always do, faster than he expects, because I always can. I'll be wrecked afterward, and it'll feel like always…for a while. And then it won't. I'll head upstairs and Isaac won't be there.

I'm not "fine" with any of it. But it's like, if my arm stroke needs improving, Mr. Watkins doesn't give me a couple of rest days and hope it all gets better. No, he makes me dive back in and swim until I get it right. I have to train. Same principle here. I can't just sit on the couch. I need to dive back in. I need to train myself to be fine with this.

Mom says, "If you're adamant, you can go in."

So long as…

"So long as…"

There we go.

"…you sit down with Tony."

She means Mr. Ford. "No."

"He can decide whether you're fine or not."

"*No.*"

"Or you can take the day off."

"Or…" I don't have an alternative—I'm buying some time before it smashes into me. "*Or* I can go to Squad, do that, then come up to the English staff room for my free first period, and we can hang."

Mom reaches for more broccoli. "The sophomores have an assessment," she says. "I've told the staff I'll duck in and check on each class, but that's fifteen minutes, max."

"Then it works?"

She nods. "It works."

"Great."

I continue eating with Mom still watching me. "You're not wild on the idea of seeing Tony, are you?"

"Nope."

"Not even if he comes here?"

"Nope."

When Mom has other work friends over for dinner or drinks by the pool, they're not like they are at school. I mean, I've always seen behind the curtain, but after three margaritas, the curtain doesn't exist. They're real people who live full, crazy lives. Not Mr. Ford. He's never not the school counselor. I don't even think he likes Mom first-naming him in front of me.

And he's a land mine.

"If the school says you boys have to go see him, do you want me to get you out of it?"

"Please."

It's Mr. Ford's job to listen more than he speaks, to hear what's said and to realize what isn't. I have too much to hide from someone whose job it is to find out.

Who's also friends with my mom.

Land mine.

"All right, I'll tell them we have a family counselor," Mom says.

"That makes us sound nuts."

"Ryan!"

"What? It does."

Mom doesn't argue. "I'll think of something." She

crosses the room and hesitates. "I'm going to have a bath. Will you be all right?"

I glance down at my overloaded plate. "I'm sure I'll manage."

"You know what I mean."

"I'm good." I smile a little, because Mom needs me to. "Thanks."

———

I tell her I'm going for a jog. It's not a lie, but not the full truth either. She says I should rest. I say I won't go far. She wants to convince me to stay but she knows I'm already gone.

"Take your phone," is all that's left.

I start down the street. My cell phone swings like a pendulum in the mesh pocket now drooping past the end of my running shorts. It's a fantastic look.

I don't like jogging. It aggravates my left knee in a way swimming never does. But it gets me where I need to be, and it explains where I've been.

I've perfected the route. There's one backstreet that almost takes me right from my house down to the water. Then I join the coastal track that snakes from Bondi Beach down south. There are stairs carved from stone. This is the portion of the jog where I question whether anyone is really worth it. Morale is at its lowest and the air starts to scratch at my lungs. But it's all downhill from here, in a good way, as the path curves in line with the coast until: my omission.

Todd sits on the edge of the cliff rock, his feet dangling off. It's not the actual edge—there's a six-foot drop to the next bit of cliff and then a steeper drop to broken bones. *That's* the real edge. This is edge lite.

He isn't how I imagined my first boyfriend—a surfer with an on-the-nose name like Sandy, knotted blond hair and sun-kissed skin—but my heart beats differently around Todd. He knows it too. He's studying premed this year, and I bought him a stethoscope for Christmas.

I sit beside him. The ocean marches from the horizon, tripping over itself under a purple sky.

Todd bounces against me softly. "Hey."

We meet each other halfway. I live in Bellevue Hill, he lives in Coogee, and this is roughly the middle. Usually, he brings his day, I bring mine, and we exchange them.

I've left my day at home. I just want this, us and an infinite sea.

There's no one coming along the path, so I rest my head on his shoulder and close my eyes. My hand falls onto his. His skin is warm. I start tracing swirls over his fingers, then trace the letters of the words I can't bring myself to say.

I miss Isaac already.

And then, more swirls, as if I can bury my confession underneath them. I relax deeper into his shoulder. I hear him breathing through his nose and feel his body expand and contract. I smile.

Laughter cuts through the air. I pull away. Two brisk walkers are coming down the path from Bondi, trading jokes. I worry I moved too abruptly, but Todd doesn't react. The waves slap against the rocks below us and he doesn't say a word.

———————

Hank pulls open the staff-room door and catches a whiff of chlorine. "Come straight from the pool?" he asks, re-treating back to his workstation.

"Yeah."

"Ice cream?" he asks.

Hank's a prime example of how jarring it can be to peer behind the curtain. Out in the halls, he's Mr. Morgan, this menacing teacher who barks, "Boys!" like it's some kind of threat. In here, he's a gentle giant with a mini freezer under his desk.

"No." Mr. Watkins would kill me. "But thanks."

I shut the door.

"Suit yourself." Hank bites into his chocolate-coated ice cream. I don't get it. It isn't even nine o'clock, and the air conditioner is set to Arctic.

"Do you have a free?" I ask.

"No, I thought I'd relax in here while my eighth grad-ers reenact *Lord of the Flies*."

No other student would believe Mr. Morgan ever makes jokes.

"I'm gonna…" I point across the room. He tips his ice cream to me and swivels back to face his computer.

Each English teacher has a tiny workstation against the wall, except Mom. She has an office in the corner. When I'm there alone, she insists I keep the door open. I don't know what difference it makes; the wall is mostly glass. Anyone can look in and see what I'm doing. Not that I mind. I can think of worse places to spend first period. Like in Mr. Ford's office, or the library. At least here I can play music and access the staff wireless network, where none of the good websites are blocked.

I drop my bags in the corner and get comfortable at Mom's desk. I launch a playlist on my phone. The beat is heavy enough to make Hank look over. He doesn't need to say a word. I pause the track. "Sorry," I mouth.

He returns to his work. I find a silent way to pass the time: making sense of the scrawled notes Mom's stuck to everything on her desk. When the staff-room door opens, I expect it to be her. It's Amy. Mom has mixed feelings about Amy. She always looks like she's received bad news; Mom can't stand that, but she knows the impact of a young female face on male minds.

Amy leans back on the door until it closes. She stays there for a moment, blinking up at the ceiling.

"Forget something?" Hank asks.

Amy shakes her head. "No, but I told them I did."

Her face screws up like she's willing herself not to cry. Hank launches out of his chair. He pulls her in close and consoles her, angling the ice cream away from her cardigan.

I'm not supposed to be seeing this, but Hank's forgotten I'm here.

Amy says, "I had to skip over his name on the roll."

My chest tightens. Amy teaches Isaac's class. She's fresh out of college; he must be her first...

The hairs on the back of my neck stand on end.

Inhale.

Exhale.

"Do you want me to pop in and look after them for a bit?" he asks Amy, releasing her.

"No, no, it's fine." She wipes her eyes. "I'll be fine." She clears her throat and straightens her blouse. "I doubt they feel any better." She grabs a whiteboard marker off the nearest shelf. "Can't go back without something."

She leaves and Hank closes the door. He turns and our eyes meet. I must look shattered, because his shoulders drop. He shrinks.

"Ryan," he says.

Inhale.

Exhale.

I loop my arm through the straps of my bags and make a break for the door. "I just remembered…" My eyes sting. I blink. "I have this thing. Tell Mom, everything's fine."

And I'm out. I cross the hall, take the fire stairs two at a time and charge out onto the lower level. The hallway's deserted. Anyone else with a free first isn't stupid enough to be in yet. That's one of the perks of Squad. I'm in at the crack of dawn, no matter what.

My locker isn't far from the stairwell. Blinking back tears, I enter my combination. I pull down; it doesn't unlock. "Damn you." I reset the lock with three twists of the dial and try again, slower this time. It works.

I can't shake the thought of Amy standing against the

door, breaking. I want to cry for her. I want to cry for me. I want to cry for Isaac.

Maybe coming back so soon was a mistake.

I open my locker. The bolt-cutters are propped up against the corner.

I completely forgot about the *other* stuff that happened yesterday. Raiding Isaac's locker. The money. Miles. He and Isaac were up to something, and whatever it was, I helped cover it up. The proof is still in my locker.

I need to get rid of it. I breathe out the emotional residue and focus. Bolt-cutters. Right. I have to return them to Mr. Collins's office before he realizes they are gone. He probably has a class now. Amy's definitely back in her classroom. I wonder how she's—

I exhale.

There's whistling. I wipe my eyes and peer over. A maintenance guy in a baggy collared tee shuffles up the hallway, a ladder under one arm. I cram my stuff into my locker, concealing the bolt-cutters. He continues past but doesn't get far. He turns the ladder upright and unfolds it like a pro. He climbs up and starts tinkering with something on the ceiling.

My bag sinks forward, exposing the blades. Quickly, I angle my body between the maintenance guy and my locker. I unzip my sports bag and slip the bolt-cutters inside.

"What's that, now?"

I almost jump out of my skin. I look back. The maintenance guy's on the phone, standing beneath the exposed wiring of a security camera.

"Hang on—don't. I'll be right up." He ends the call with a string of obscenities, then notices me watching. "I didn't say any of that."

"None of it," I concur.

He holds a small black dome against the ceiling and starts screwing it back on. Looking past him, I see the same black domes dot the ceiling at regular intervals. There's one near Isaac's locker.

The school has footage of us breaking in.

———

I'm late for Modern History, even with a free beforehand. It's a skill. I shut the door quietly behind me.

"You're early!" Omar snorts.

Shut up, Omar.

Mr. Butler feels the same way. "Shut up, Omar." His eyes follow me as I weave between the desks. "Nice of you to join us, Ryan. Work is on the board. Get started."

Isaac always sat between Miles and me. Today, Miles has filled the void with a stack of library books. He's an aggressive borrower. The moment we learn our next Modern History topic, he checks every relevant book out of the library. I doubt he even uses them.

I approach. He doesn't tear his eyes away from his school planner when he says, "Hey."

He has no idea how much shit we're in.

"Mr. Ford told me Isobel is coming in to collect Isaac's stuff." He's congratulating himself. We got into the locker before them. He thinks we've won.

"There are cameras."

Miles looks up. "What?"

"I checked. In the halls, outside Mr. Collins's office, near Isaac's locker, everywhere," I say. "They saw everything."

Miles leans closer. "Someone spoke to you?"

"No, but—"

He shrugs it off. "Then we are fine. They are only there for when there is an incident."

I blink hard. "You knew?"

My surprise bounces off him. "They are difficult to miss. Honestly, I would not be surprised if they were empty shells put there to scare us."

"They're not. I saw a maintenance guy fixing one and… You let me break into a teacher's office and then Isaac's locker, knowing there were cameras?"

He blinks. There's no remorse.

"You're unbelievable," I say.

"Relax. No one is going to check the footage for no reason."

I want to counter his point but I can't. He's right. Nobody saw us. There'd be no reason to check the footage. I mean, Mr. Butler whacked the front of Mom's car and she had to chase down the surveillance footage. I exhale. We're in the clear. We got in and out before—

"Isobel," I mutter.

"Yes, before lunch," Miles says.

"No, no, she's coming to open the locker. Mr. Collins will realize he doesn't have the bolt-cutters."

There's a raised eyebrow. "You have not put them back?"

"You left me standing in the hall holding them when the bell rang. I didn't have a chance."

"Ryan, you need to put them back."

"Really? Thanks, I hadn't pieced that together." Sarcasm everywhere.

"Ryan." It's Mr. Butler's attempt at sternness. It isn't very threatening.

"Yeah?"

"Are you going to take out your things?" he asks.

Miles's eyes flare. "Or did you leave them in your locker?"

I reach for my bag. "No, I've got them right—" Oh, I get what he means. "Actually, sir, I need to go to the toilet."

He's unimpressed. "You just came in."

"And I only just needed to go."

Mr. Butler sighs and shoos me off with one hand.

———

When I'm out of view, I sprint to my locker. I grab the sports bag with the bolt-cutters in it, throw it over my shoulder and hope Mr. Collins has a class. He doesn't. I can see him through the glass panel. He must sense someone standing close, because he looks up. He smiles and waves me in.

I haven't had much to do with Mr. Collins. I've never been in one of his classes and Mom's never invited him over. He works in the school boardinghouse, and beyond that, he's a total mystery. I don't even know his first name.

I open the door. He's shoving his gym gear to one side, making room on the couch. "Ryan! Sit, sit." He wheels his chair back. "Wait, do you have a free?"

I don't hesitate. "Sure."

I sink into the couch. Mr. Collins hunches over, elbows on his thighs. "How are you doing?" he asks. It's more sigh than speech.

I don't know how to answer the question. I can tell him what happened in the staff room earlier, how contagious Amy's sadness had been, how suddenly it had gripped me... But that paints a very specific picture of how I'm doing, and honestly, it hasn't been like that. Not the whole time. Can I say it's not as bad as I thought it would be? Mostly, it isn't this huge sadness. It's a constant sort of hollowness in my chest. An acknowledgment of an absence. And piled on top of that, there's the stuff I still have to worry about, like the stolen bolt-cutters in the bag on my lap.

"I'm all right," I say.

He doesn't push for an elaboration. Instead, he asks if I want a drink. "I have some OJ somewhere," he adds.

I remember seeing the packet when I was raiding his things. It's in the top drawer of his desk.

"I'm good, thanks."

"Well, I'm going to have some." He turns to his desk and pulls open the drawer. While he wrestles a juice box out of the plastic packet, I realize I have a chance. I unzip my bag and reach for—

Mr. Collins swivels back around, breaking the juice box's seal with a straw.

"Actually, could I have one?" I ask, my heart in my mouth. He's happy to oblige. He opens the drawer again and I drop the bolt-cutters onto the floor. I guide them under the desk with one foot. I'm half-off the couch when he holds the juice out to me.

I accept the orange juice and sit up. "Cramping," I explain without him asking. I glance down—the bolt-cutters' handles are poking out. Close enough. I break the box's seal and take a sip. It tastes nothing like any orange I've ever had. Still, it doesn't last long.

I should leave. I've done what I needed to, but I'm in no rush to return to the stack of books where Isaac used to be.

"Does it get any better?" I ask.

Mr. Collins lowers his drink and wheels closer. He swallows hard. "I'll probably get into trouble for saying this, but… We all pretend like we know what we're doing when it comes to this stuff, like we know how to fix what you're feeling, but we don't. We're all feeling it too." He's being too bleak, so he adds, "Time. Time helps."

I push my straw down into the empty juice box. "So you've…lost a student before?"

"When I was doing my placement, there was a freshman," Mr. Collins says.

"Oh."

"He'd been sick for a while, so it wasn't sudden, but it's always shit." He doesn't hesitate, or whisper it; he just lets *shit* land like the most adequate word, professional code of conduct be damned. I appreciate it.

"And there was—" He stops and furrows his brow, considering whether or not to share. He decides to. "My best friend died in senior year."

"How?" I blurt.

He deflects the question with a short shake of his head. I feel bad. "Sorry."

If it bothers him, he doesn't show it. "My parents were originally from Adelaide. Whenever they had the chance, they took me back. Callum and I were apart for weeks at a time and it didn't faze me. But as soon as I knew I would never see him again…I needed him. It took me a while to realize why. I was a private person, reluctant, nervous— but not with Callum. We shared everything through high school. When I lost him, I lost all that time. He was the other half of every anecdote, and the one who remembered them better. I'd put all my eggs in one basket, and suddenly…" He nods a fraction. "Callum was gone, and no amount of needing him would bring him back."

"What did you do?"

He sits back and exhales. "Well, I…" He gives it more thought. Eventually, he continues, "I don't know whether it was conscious or not, but I stopped holding back. I told people more. Even if I only knew them for a minute, I made sure they knew something about me. Instead of putting all my eggs in one basket, I put smaller eggs in many baskets. You could say I diversified my investments, protected myself from the volatility of the market. So if something happened to one basket, I had plenty more, and I'd never have to start from scratch again."

He grimaces. "It could have been me, and that scared me," he adds. "I didn't want to leave my legacy to one person and risk it being lost. I gave as much of myself to as many people, so that when they put all those pieces together, that would be the mark I left on the world."

"I'm sorry." It's all I can think to say.

"Don't be. It's… You'll find what makes it better for you. Me, I was a shy kid. It's apples and oranges."

I know what he thinks. I'm Ryan Patrick Thomson, Olympic hopeful. That's my mark, but it isn't all of me. There's so much only Isaac knew. The world is a dark place when you're hiding something. Telling Isaac who I liked, when we kissed, how it felt—that was me kicking the door open a smidge to let the light in. He was my light in dark places, and now he's gone.

The apples are apples.

"I should probably go back to class."

Mr. Collins sighs. "Why did I have a feeling you didn't actually have a free?"

"Uh…because you're in charge of the schedule?"

I can tell he wants to laugh. "Off you go."

———

Mr. Butler doesn't notice I've been gone for nearly half the period. Miles does. "Is it done?" he asks without looking up from his textbook.

"Yeah."

He turns the page and highlights a passage. The bolt-
cutters are back in Mr. Collins's office, and that resolves
everything—the cameras, the break-ins—so we don't
need to talk anymore. He's not going to tell me where
the money came from, what he and Isaac were up to,
because we're not actually friends.

It's like he's drawn a line under yesterday and moved
on. I watch him over the books stacked between us.
He's writing something in the margin of his page. I go
to speak but my chest is tight. The world is dark. I want
to kick the door down and let the light in. I want to tell
him I'm scared and sad, without being afraid of it sounding gay. And I want to tell him I kiss guys and it's awesome. I want to…not pretend. But I don't have the guts.

I need what I had with Isaac. Some light. Any light.

Mr. Collins is in my head, telling me to diversify my
investments. Smaller eggs, many baskets.

I speak up. "My favorite color is aqua."

"And?" Miles asks.

———

We have a spot that's ours, a table in the corner of the
courtyard farthest from the staff common room. Miles
would always get on my case for saying it was "furthest."
When I stopped, Harley started. He likes the way ignoring tedious grammatical distinctions makes Miles squirm.

I can almost see it playing out like it has a thousand
times. Harley sitting slouched, smugly clicking his tongue

against the roof of his mouth, Miles getting into a huff, Isaac biting back a smirk.

The paint job might be flaking and it might get the worst of the jacaranda's fury, but this table is where we orbited Isaac.

I unwrap my lunch—sushi from the caf—and wait. Two younger kids try to commandeer a corner to copy each other's homework.

"No."

"But we—"

"No."

They scoop up their books and keep walking.

This is the spot that's ours.

———

There's a nineteenth-century drawing room in the back of our English classroom—think comfortable chair, world globe and antique bookshelf all on a rug tucked in the corner. It's mostly for ambience, to give the room a scholarly feel, but Conrad sits back there to raise productivity. We can't see him, so we assume he's always watching.

I check over my shoulder. He *is* watching. I fake dusting something off my shirt and turn back. Hank's told Mom what happened in the staff room, that's a certainty. She hasn't sent a message or come to find me, which means Conrad's her eyes and ears. She'll grill him the moment class is over.

I should at least look productive.

I open my English folder and thumb through the pages. I get to a sheet explaining literary techniques and lose my breath. Isaac wrote over the top of it. His letters are tall and thin: What You Need Right Now. Underlined twice in red, because presentation was important to him. He thought that as the son of the head of English, I didn't abuse my power nearly enough, so he compiled a list of excuses guaranteed to get me out of class (ranging from imminent bowel movements to personal tragedies) and instructions on how to make a selection *(just close your eyes and fucking point at one).*

My English clashed with his Business Studies. He had an identical list of excuses on the inside of his textbook cover. If either of us wanted to bail, we'd text. We'd hang in the bathroom near our lockers and end up laughing so hard I'm surprised we were never caught.

I'm smiling. It still feels like an option. I close my eyes and circle my index finger over the page. I plant it down and reopen my eyes.

I turn in my seat. "Sir, I left my Shakespeare in my locker." Not one of his funnier ones, I'll admit.

We're twenty minutes into the lesson. Any other day, I'm certain Conrad would have berated me.

"Go on, then."

I take the familiar route, down one flight of stairs and then left. There's a small gathering outside Isaac's locker. My chest hollows out. Isobel is clearing out the last of his things, flanked by Mrs. Evans. Mr. Collins is holding a garbage bag.

Isobel always existed on the edges of our friendship.

She answered the door, rolled her eyes when Isaac said something I'd snigger at. She's older, somewhere after college but before a job she doesn't hate—too old to have any time for guys our age.

She turns something over in her hands, assessing its value. I can't tell what it is from this far, but she eventually drops it into Mr. Collins's garbage bag. She takes up something else and turns it over. She pauses. Her chest rises. Her chest falls. She stashes it in the sports bag by her feet.

"That's it, then," she says.

I don't wait for them to notice me. I dart back up the stairs.

———

In the time it takes to buy my lunch, a pack of eighth graders claim the spot that's ours. Miles would always arrive first, spread out his books and mark the territory till we got here. I guess, without him and Harley, the spot isn't really ours anymore. I wonder where they are, how they spend their lunches and if they'll ever come back. Maybe like Isobel, they've sorted the treasure from the trash, kept what's needed and tossed the rest.

I eat my lunch elsewhere.

———

"I didn't hear you come in," Mom says, standing in my bedroom doorway.

Lying on the bed, I tell her, "I'm a ninja."

She crosses the room. I expect her to say something about the chlorine smell or the leaning tower of unfolded clothes, like the reality of living with me is surprising. Instead, she asks how swimming was. I tell her it was fine. There isn't much I can say about Squad, especially after so many years. There was water. It was wet.

"Shove over." I roll a little to make room for her on the bed. She sits up against the headboard and massages my scalp with her fingertips. "Sorry I missed you this morning."

When she asks if I'm okay, I say, "Not really."

She's quiet. I wonder if she expected bravado. Her fingers still. "We had a staff meeting today. They've made the funeral arrangements—it'll be in the chapel on Thursday during fourth period. Your whole class is going. You can spend the morning beforehand in my office, if you like. And they've given me the afternoon off, so we'll come straight back here."

"All right."

"Do you have homework?"

I nod.

"Do you want to watch a movie?"

I nod.

———————

Only nine of us take Health, but Richo insists on calling the roll instead of counting. A mountain in a tracksuit, hunched over a tiny laptop, he works through the alphabet. Cooper Adams and Thom Foley answer their names with, "Sir."

"Scott Harley?" The room is quiet. Richo looks around. "Anybody seen Harley?"

I haven't, come to think of it. Not since leaving the chapel on Monday.

When no one answers, Richo peers back down at his screen. "Right. Absent."

In the front row, Marty Johnson mimes knocking back a beer.

———

At Squad, we're told to stay present. I try to. When I dive, I'm alert, aware of every movement and its effect. My form is my priority and every stroke has power. I follow the black tiled line to the opposite wall and repeat and repeat and then my brain changes channel. I think of Harley. I think of Miles. I think of myself. What does it say about us if we're still at school and Harley isn't? Are we stronger, or did Isaac mean less to us?

I stop at the wall, pull my goggles up and check the clock in the corner. An hour to go.

"Time's crawling today." Two lanes over, Peanut's on the rope.

This is his second year on the Squad. We swim laps. We wake up too early to swim them and suffer the same diet to swim them better. We have hours of life in common, and I don't even know his real name. I recognize him from his photo on the allergy wall in the staff common room, though. Peanut.

"Part of me wants to bail and get Collins to write me a note," he adds.

It takes me a second to put it together. Peanut's a boarder, so Mr. Collins can get him out of training. That means he must know how Harley is. I ask him.

He scratches his nose and lowers his goggles. "Haven't seen him. He left on Monday."

"Left where?"

He shrugs. "TITF." He inhales deeply and pushes off the wall.

———

I empty my pockets onto the coffee table—wrappers, wallet, coins, phone. *Phone.* I check it.

MOM
Where are you?

I forgot to text her. Shit.

ME
I'm at Miles's place for dinner. Didn't I tell you?

Her reply is instant.

MOM
No.

When I lie to her, I always read so deeply into her responses that one-word messages like that feel pregnant with meaning. She doesn't believe me. She knows I'm hiding something. She's going to drive to Miles's and find I'm not there.

Todd calls from inside.

"What?" I'm still staring at my cell phone.

ME
Sorry. I thought I did.

Todd emerges from around the corner. He's holding a bottle of sauce. "Barbecue?"

"Ketchup, if you've got any."

He open-mouth smiles. All my texting anxiety melts away in a heart thump. "Sure." He disappears back into the kitchen. "I *think* these steaks are done," he calls.

My phone vibrates.

MOM
Okay.

Todd's folks are in Canberra overnight and Mom thinks I'm at Miles's. It isn't much of an opportunity but it is one, and we don't have many. It's a night of small rebellions: we eat dinner on the couch; we leave our dirty plates stacked on the floor; Todd leans in and kisses me softly.

I interrupt it. "Down here?" I ask. He lives in one of those showy houses on the water where the entire wall is window. Anyone doing the coastal walk can peer straight in.

Todd stays close. "My parents won't be back tonight."

He smirks and leans in again, and all I can think about is the window. It isn't enough of a partition between out there and in here, and I pull away.

"It's fine, seriously," Todd says. "They know anyway."

I tense up and Todd feels it.

"About me," he clarifies. I knew that. "Don't worry, no one knows about you. And if they did, my parents are cool. Like, they want to meet someone I'm dating." He walks it back a bit. "Not saying you have to do it now, but whenever you're ready. It'd be nice not to have to wait for Dad to have a conference. And we could go clubbing."

"Clubbing?"

"Yeah."

"With your parents?"

"I meant *also*," he says. "When it's less secret, we can go out."

"You can. You're eighteen."

"I know a place that doesn't card."

I picture it. Dancing up against Todd to a song that's probably about dancing in a club. Green strobe lights slicing the air around us like a music video. Having to shout in each other's ears. Laughing. His hands sliding around my waist. People *noticing*.

"Me and you and a room filled with randoms is probably the one thing scarier than meeting your parents," I say.

He brushes it off. "When you're out, you don't care

about anyone but yourself…and the handsome guy you're with." He presses into me and I go with it, surrendering into the couch.

"Wait, are you calling yourself handsome?" I ask.

"I was speaking generally." He pecks me quickly. "Wait, are you saying I'm not handsome?"

I'm smiling. "Not at all."

The couch is made of two separate halves. One half starts to shift away. It's like hooking up on continental drift.

"Some guys I met at orientation are taking me out on Friday, like a pre–Mardi Gras thing. Come. You can crash here, on the couch. Mom won't mind."

"I have a swim meet after school."

"We won't go in till later."

"And I've got training on Saturday morning."

"Skip it and swim later."

"I dunno…"

"Think about it."

He kisses me again and I worry about the window.

———

I toss my bags in the corner of Mom's office and recline back into her seat. I run my thumb against my fingers; they feel like someone else's. There's an email open on her computer detailing funeral arrangements. I look everywhere else. Conrad plays Tchaikovsky in the other room. He bumps into Hank on his way out to second period. Hank asks about the grading criteria for the eighth-grade assessment. Conrad says he'll forward it when he gets to class. Hank raids the freezer when he's gone. He works in silence. I miss the Tchaikovsky. Eventually, there's the xylophone. Recess brings with it rumors of homemade chocolate muffins in the staff common room. Mom brings two.

"Eat these," she says. She places two chocolate mini muffins on the desk. One topples over.

"I can't." Empty calories. Not allowed.

"Mr. Watkins isn't your mother. Eat. And get dressed."

I didn't bother with my tie after swimming. Or shoes.

"You all right?"

"Yeah."

"You seem…"

The xylophone, again.

"I swear, break feels shorter every day," Mom says. "I'll be back at the end of third—be ready."

I watch the staff room clear out. Every teacher leaves for class and I'm left alone. With every second that passes, Isaac's funeral gets that little bit closer. I eat both muffins.

Hank and Elise return after a long break. They retreat to their stations, absorbed in their work. When Amy enters, it's with a duffel bag in hand and a new outfit. She's changed into a three-quarter black dress. She has Isaac's English class fourth, which means she's escorting them to the funeral.

"You look great," Elise says, preempting Amy's doubt.

"Really?"

Elise nods. "I don't own anything that pretty."

"Neither do I. It's my sister's." Amy scratches at the

fabric over her abdomen. "You know, sometimes I wish I was a lesbian. My wardrobe would seriously double."

I can't imagine ever sharing clothes with Todd. We have distinct styles. He dresses like a skinny lumberjack, and I roll out of bed ready for the beach. What works on him definitely wouldn't on me. And besides, guy couples who dress the same freak me out. It's like watching brothers kiss.

"You'd have more clothes, sure, but at what cost?" Elise asks.

"My soul, probably."

Elise laughs but not in the way someone laughs at a joke. She and Amy take their faith very seriously, and while most Barton teachers check their phones during the prayers at assembly, they close their eyes and mouth the words. Their strain of Christianity has a distinct "No, you can't sit with us" vibe. When Amy says loving a woman will tarnish her soul, she means it. And when Elise laughs, she's laughing at the people who don't have a seat at their table.

I can't bear to hear what's coming next. I reach for my tie and make a beeline for the exit.

"Are you going to get ready?" Amy asks.

She isn't uncomfortable I heard. She doesn't think she said anything wrong.

I nod.

———

I open the bathroom door with my shoulder. Miles is standing at the sink, combing his hair back. Weird how

Barton can be so large and feel so small sometimes. I've never been all that interested in Miles. Sounds harsh, but nobody is ever interested in their Miles. But something's different now. Since Monday, I've become interested. Since the money, I've been curious. What were he and Isaac up to? Where does he go at lunch? Are those two questions related? I can't ask, though, not now. We're not actually friends. But I ought to say something. I approach the tap beside his. "Hey."

"Hello."

Neither of us asks how the other is. We already know.

His hair is neat, but he runs his comb through it again anyway. I look down at the unmade tie hanging around my neck.

True fact: I can't tie a Windsor when someone's watching. I work through the steps as always, only it comes out too long, with a knot that's too small and tight.

I undo it and try again.

Miles speaks. "Do you ever worry about getting depression?" He asks it plainly, like it isn't heavy or personal. "I mean, we are sad now, but are you worried you might get stuck?" He places down his comb. "I am."

If I keep perfectly still, will the conversation keep going without my intervention?

"And how long are we supposed to be sad for?" he continues. "What is normal? What is expected of us?"

"There's no grading criteria for grief." I can't help myself.

"No." He swallows hard. "There is not, is there?"

Miles and I started out in the same seventh-grade class,

but I lacked initiative. I was dropped to the B class after the midterms, and when I didn't find initiative there, I was dropped again the next year. I never did find initiative, but fingers crossed, any day now...

I pull apart my knot again.

"Do you need help with that?" He's watching me in the mirror.

"No, it's fine." That was too proud, too blunt. "Thanks, though."

"From here, it looks like—"

I pivot. "Do you have a free?"

"Chemistry."

"I have French."

He cocks an eyebrow. "You can speak French?"

"*Je* cannot, no." I snort a laugh. He smiles a bit.

It reminds me of the conversations we used to have at the bench, filling time when Isaac wasn't around. The only person missing is Harley.

"Hey, question. Have you heard anything from Harley?"

Miles shakes his head. "He has not even posted on Isaac's profile."

I haven't either. I don't do social media—it's too much of a minefield. I had a profile. I put up a photo once with Mom in it, and it was this whole thing. Because she's a teacher, she can't have a visible private life, so blah, blah. Whatever, it's just easier to live off-line.

"Are people doing that?" I ask.

"Some."

"I wouldn't know what to write. For this to happen to Isaac of all people… It's so unlucky."

Miles turns from the mirror to look at me for real. "Unlucky? You cannot chalk it up to the randomness of the universe, Ryan. He had a problem."

"A problem?"

"You know what I mean."

"I really don't." Plenty of guys do what Isaac did. They're still here.

"I have never been to a gathering, not one," Miles says, more softly. "I hear parts of stories and I have seen enough movies to fill in the gaps, and I know I should feel like I am missing out. As if to be a teenager is to get plastered, wrecked, blitzed—whatever the right words are. But that just scares me. Isaac would tell me I was boring." His chest swells. "I was the only one who spoke up, Ryan. The only one."

I try to get a word in. "Look, I rarely did any of that stuff."

"Because of swimming. But you were still there. And do not get me started on Harley."

He looks back at his reflection and all I can hear is my heart beating a cappella. He's blaming us.

"Hey, wait, you can't—"

"You two never stopped him. It was *harmless*. It was *fun*. You all hung out in backyards and parks and did whatever you did, tricking each other into thinking you were invincible."

My heart's on fire, slamming hard against my chest.

Miles slips his comb into the breast pocket of his blazer. "I should get back to class."

He crosses the room, and I feel I need to say something to defend Isaac. He wasn't an idiot. He didn't have a problem. He was unlucky, plain and simple.

"They must've sold him junk," I blurt out. "He didn't know what he was getting."

Miles stops in the doorway. He deflates. "He did not need what they were giving."

The door closes softly behind him.

———

Mom grabs a program by the door and I follow her inside. When I'm in the chapel, I always feel like I'm wading through a presence. I haven't believed in God since I was old enough to pray for something and not get it, so I don't think it's Him. It's probably the million prayers with nowhere else to go.

The librarians are saving us a spot. When we pass Mr. Butler, Mom stops to embrace him. She coos something supportive in his ear. It's funny how a coffin can change what people think of each other.

I try not to stare at it, but it's magnetic. It's a profound loose end, every unresolved conversation, unfulfilled plan. The Robertses sit close to it. Isobel and her dad are dressed in black, looking down at their laps. Between them, Mrs. Roberts looks over her shoulder. She's wearing a psychedelic tie-dyed shirt. I immediately recognize it as Isaac's. Her face is hollow and her eyes are wide. Her pupils sweep the room, which is close to full now. She takes a staggered breath and her gaze lands on me. She holds it.

Our shared history replays. All at once, she's driving us from school for my first sleepover at Isaac's, casually probing for details about my life; she's standing behind him, running her fingers through his hair while he eats his breakfast until he nags her to stop; she's fanning the smoke away from the beeping detector with a tea towel after our failed attempt to cook dinner… Isobel whispers something in her ear and she turns back to the front of the chapel.

"The photos in the program are nice," Mom says.

It barely registers. Mom must feel my distance. She grabs my hand. I look at her and she says she loves me. I count to twenty before I free my hand to check my phone.

A message from Todd. I angle the screen so Mom can't see.

TODD
Thinking of you. X

Brother Mitchell starts proceedings. He welcomes guests to the school and to his chapel and invites us to stand for the first hymn. "Isaac was such a fan of hymns," he says with the roughness of a former chain-smoker. "I know he gave some staff members trouble…" He pauses for grief-tinged laughter, "but I have never seen a boy his age so committed to belting out a hymn."

Isaac's love of hymns stemmed from his love of un-intended sexual innuendo. Brother Mitchell knows this. He's made the selection accordingly. "Have Thine Own Way, Lord" is a laugh factory. I snigger partway through the first line.

"Don't," Mom whispers, lips curled into a smile.

The room is largely playing it straight. I notice a guy standing in the back row in a hoodie and well-worn jeans. There are dark rings around his eyes. He chews on his thumbnail. Harley.

Our gazes meet. I nod and he gives me nothing.

"Turn around," Mom urges, before committing to the final line of the song. "You know," she adds as we both sit, "it's not a bad song."

"Mm." Harley's thrown me.

Mrs. Roberts walks to the pulpit. She clears her throat and lays a crisp sheet of paper down in front of her. She doesn't consult it.

She walks us through Isaac's life—the first steps, the first stern call from a teacher, the first girlfriend. I haven't heard these stories before. Isaac was so fully formed by the time we became friends in fifth grade. While the rest of us tumbled through adolescence, he was already eighteen, just going through the motions until every-one else caught up.

Mrs. Roberts's speech ends suddenly. She consults her paper—that's all she's written. She looks back up and soaks in the audience. She takes a breath.

"There are so many of Isaac's peers here, and...I want to say Isaac lived a full life and retroactively justify him not being here by saying he lived more in his sixteen years than most ever would, but that isn't true. He didn't live enough, he didn't love enough, he didn't see enough, and if there's a lesson in all this—do more. You don't know how long you have. Do what makes you happy. Live, love and be remarkable."

Her words linger.

She clears her throat once more. "Thank you all for being here. To see so many of his friends… I know it was mandatory. He would have liked that."

Everybody laughs. She consults the program and adds, "I think there's another hymn now…" Brother Mitchell rises, and there's an awkward back-and-forth about who should introduce the song. "Oh, I can do it," Mrs. Roberts says.

She does. The organ starts and the room is slow to its feet. I check back on Harley. He's struggling with the door. He opens it wide enough to escape. The music masks the door shutting behind him.

Mom nudges me and I turn back. She has the program open between us. Everyone starts singing. Mom's mumbling the words and I'm looking past the lyrics. It says Mrs. Evans is scheduled to speak next.

I can miss that. I ought to.

I squeeze past the others in our row and ignore Mom asking where I'm going. I power walk down the aisle and heave the door open. I expect Harley on the other side of it.

The hallway is empty.

He's bailed. I sprint past reception, out the door, down the front steps and through the gate. The street pavement is swollen with businesspeople on their way to lunch. I turn, hoping for a glimpse of Harley's hood, a teenage blip on a corporate radar. Nothing.

———

The doorbell goes off a second time. Mom waits for me to descend the stairs before she opens up. The way she bellows, "Hello!" it's like she hasn't seen Hank today, or every other school day. I try not to roll my eyes. It's been just the two of us long enough for me to spot her schemes a mile off. Apparently she and Hank made dinner plans for tonight a while ago. Yeah, and I'm a unicorn. I appreciate it, though. The pageantry of a staff dinner will keep tonight from being a total downer.

"And you brought Jonathan!" Mom's quick to embrace the second man to cross the threshold. When she pulls back, she prompts me. "Ryan, you remember Hank's roommate?"

"Yeah." I shake their hands.

"I hope you don't mind," Hank says. "I mentioned I was coming, and he remembers Christmas."

Jonathan lights up. "That meal was sublime."

"Well, adjust your expectations," Mom warns. "I didn't make a turkey."

"You haven't had long to prepare," I tease.

"I've had weeks." She's committed to the story, I'll give her that much.

She leads us past the blue glass-tile feature wall. Hank says he loves what we've done to modernize the place. Mom tells him to shut up. He laughs.

When she gets to the kitchen, she fetches a third glass and starts pouring. The first bottle of red doesn't last very long, so the adults leap from polite dinner conversation to "I can't believe you said that in front of Ryan" in record time.

"Nothing leaves this table." Mom gestures wildly, as if which table she was referring to could be a point of future contention.

I cross my heart with one finger.

"You'll understand, one day."

Oh, I understand red wine.

I smirk down at my cleared plate. I'm still hungry, but my seconds are Jonathan's firsts.

He picks at my food slowly. "In the car over, Hank was explaining Twelvies," he says.

"Twelvies?" Mom asks.

"The younger kids who act tough," Hank says. "I look at them and think, *You're twelve. I could break you. Grow up.*"

Mom nods. "Oh."

"That's the good thing about living with a teacher," Jonathan says. "You're always learning."

Jonathan bounces against Hank softly. It reminds me of Todd.

———

I call out to Mom on her way past my bedroom.

She stops. *"Mm?"*

My mouth is suddenly dry. "Hank and Jonathan, they're more than roommates, aren't they?"

She drags her feet as she approaches. She tells me to move over and I do. She sits up against the headboard.

"It's delicate," she says eventually. "The school has policies and if they were more than housemates, it would cause…difficulties."

I tilt my head back at her. "Would they fire him?"

She lowers her chin into her chest. Her gaze wavers as she finds the right phrasing. "There'd be pressure. The school would never own the decision, though. They'd blame *conservative parents*."

"And you've known awhile?"

She laughs. "Hon, I knew when I hired him." Her eyes meet mine. "Your mom's a sharp cookie. Not much gets past her."

I feel like the subject's changed. She's looking at me and she knows. No, she can't… My chest tightens. I've been careful. But I was careful and Todd noticed me. She knows. She *knows*… And the panic melts. There's relief. I can kick the door down and let the light in. No more hiding, no more retreating to the shadows, only standing in the sun. Only. Everything will be scrutinized. There'll be…difficulties.

What of them? I'll have Mom. I want what Hank and Jonathan have, but not exactly that. I want a partner, not a roommate.

And this is my chance.

I go to speak and Mom speaks first. "As much as I can't wait for you to bring a girl home so I have an excuse to entertain, playing host exhausts me."

I exhale. "Oh."

She pecks the side of my forehead. "I need to go to sleep."

Mom pushes off the bed and on her way out, I say her name. She turns; I hesitate.

"Good night," I add.

———————

Squad's always light the morning of a meet. If anybody's going to lose by an arm's length tonight, there's no amount of morning prep that will change it. We're here because we always are, devout believers in the back-and-forth. Dive, break the water—*shit, it's freezing*—tumble turn, swim back, find a rhythm, tumble, tumble, back, forth, back, forth.

Back. Mom pushes off the bed and on her way out, I say her name.

Forth. She barely turns before I blurt it. It's not poetic or careful, just the truth: "I'm gay." Her gaze softens, like it wounds her.

No, that isn't right.

Back. Mom pushes off the bed and on her way out, I say her name.

Forth. She turns. I take a breath, and on the exhale, I tell her what I've owed her. She smiles like she already knows. She invites Todd over for lunch on Sunday. He squeezes my hand on the table, not under it. He takes me to the movies and kisses me before they dim the lights. Someone mutters, "Fags."

I tumble.

Back. He takes me to the movies and kisses me before they dim the lights.

Forth. No one says a word. He comes to a swim meet. I introduce him to the team. They turn away from me in the showers. I'm the gay one now.

I don't want them to look at me and see a rainbow, but is it any better that they look at me and see a lie?

I go back and forth.

———

Mr. Watkins says I don't need to race today. He doesn't get it. I'm not doing this for the school.

When they call my race, I approach my starting block. I lower the goggles. We step onto the blocks in unison.

Twenty-four seconds is all I need.

On my mark.

The gun fires. I launch into the water and I rebuild my life, piece by piece, stroke by stroke. I seize the lead and keep it. I push myself harder. They can't take this.

I touch. First. I collapse against the wall. Every inhale is violent. The timekeeper congratulates me. 23.89 seconds.

The guy in the lane beside mine nods. I look past him to the cheering Barton contingent. Joys of a home meet, they're half the crowd. And I'm their champion. I'm Ryan Patrick Thomson, Olympic hopeful.

That is certain.

My heart thumps against my naked chest.

"You can still come tonight, if you want." There's a hopeful nervousness in Todd's voice.

My heart sinks. Dinner's my way of avoiding tonight without feeling like a flake. We sit with our legs over the edge, eating grilled fish and rice. It isn't a night out clubbing. He doesn't get to introduce me to his friends.

Like all compromises, it comes up short.

I'm not ready to be introduced as somebody's boyfriend. Instead of saying that, I tell him I'm tired, that after the week I've had, I want to hibernate all weekend.

I feel bad, hiding behind Isaac like that.

Todd's smile is warm. "No worries. Thought I'd try again."

He bounces against me. I think of Hank and Jonathan, and Mom walking out of my bedroom without me saying anything.

"I almost came out to Mom last night," I say. "She invited this teacher over for dinner. He's gay, which was news to me. He brought his boyfriend and it was a fun night. Afterward, Mom and I were talking about it, and she said something about not much getting past her. I don't know if I read too much into it, but lying there, I thought it was her telling me she knew, encouraging me to say something to confirm it. But I didn't. My chance was right there and I didn't take it."

"Why not?"

I'm gay. I'm sure of it, but I'm scared of it. Once I say

it, I'll be in that box forever. I tell him. "I don't want to be seen as the gay kid."

Todd's reply is swift. "But you are, though."

"It's complicated."

He tilts his head. "Is it?"

"I don't want to be just that."

"Am I just that?"

I can feel the conversation slipping away from me. "No, I…I don't know."

We're both quiet. I scoop some rice but stop myself. My appetite is gone.

Todd speaks up. "I won't lie—some people will see you as just that. It's inevitable. But you can't live your life for them. They aren't worth knowing, let alone living for. I came out one—"

"Month after you first kissed a guy." I've heard it before.

"That's about as long as I could handle hiding it," he continues. "I know you want to find the right time, I get that, but there isn't one. As much as I can't handle it, I'm hiding again, because of you, Ryan. I don't want to pressure you, but…" He abandons it.

The ocean laps against the rocks.

"*But* what?"

"It's nothing… It's… There's only so much longer I can wait."

———

I collapse onto the carpet, wrecked. Nothing strips my mind like working my core. But as my breathing steadies and the burn in my abs fades, our message history pops back into my head. I turn to the left, to my phone face-down on the floor. Todd hasn't replied. I would have heard it if he had.

I draw my belly button in and start over. One. I lift up off the floor. Hold for one, down for two. Two. Core tight, I lift myself again, hold for one, down for two. Three. I focus on the count until I lose count. Then there's just the burn and my strength to push through it. One builds, the other depletes, until I collapse onto the carpet, wrecked.

I see Todd sitting on the edge and telling me my time is running out. My phone pulls my focus. I texted him before lunch. Surely he's replied. I just haven't heard it.

I snatch up the phone.

ME

Have fun tonight.

Read 4:05 PM

His battery's dead. Obviously. It's Mardi Gras. It's a big day. He's out early, taking a million pics. I check his feed. I don't have an account, but I know his username. His last pic was uploaded ten minutes ago. He's standing on the curb, beaming, dressed as an '80s pro wrestler. He's a string bean busting out of fluorescent tights. It's as funny as he said it would be.

His battery isn't dead; he just hasn't replied.

It's hard not to feel crappy.

I see myself beside him, beaming, busting out of my

own fluorescent tights. He has his arm around my waist. He pecks my cheek in time for the photo. We watch the parade, drinking vodka lemonade from water bottles. He takes my hand and leads me to a club. The strobe lights slice the air. We dance close. My eyes catch his. And then we kiss.

I'm on my bedroom floor, the taste of what he's drinking almost on my lips.

I wish I could call Isaac. Words would bounce between us, and even if nothing really changed afterward, I'd feel better. Now my words have nowhere to go. I think of him and see the coffin. And I hear his mom saying he didn't live enough.

You don't know how long you have. Do what makes you happy.

I can tell Mom I'm going to Miles's for help with homework, say I'm staying the night. It's too late to match Todd's costume, but I have a uniform I've outgrown. I was supposed to donate it to the school clothing pool years ago. It'll do.

Live, love and be remarkable.

I launch off the floor and slide my wardrobe open. The uniform hangs in the corner—white shirt, dark gray shorts. I toss them on and check myself in the mirrored door. I look like a schoolkid. I pull the shirt over my shoulders, grab my scissors and cut it three buttons shorter. I try it on again. The lower half of my eight-pack and swimmer's V are exposed. Now, *that's* a pride costume.

I exhale. It looks gay. I think it like it's a bad thing.

But gay is my hand slipping into Todd's lap in the movie theater. Gay is kicking our feet over the edge. I like gay; I am gay.

I force myself to think it again.

It looks gay.

It still feels like an insult. I try again.

I look gay.

Again.

I like being gay.

"I like being gay," I repeat out loud. I smile at my reflection.

"Ryan," Mom says.

My heart slams against my chest. My lungs shatter. I gasp for air and look to the door. It's closed. Mom isn't standing there. But I heard her. I— The intercom. I slump forward and exhale in bursts. I'm relieved, depleted. She hasn't seen me like this.

Click. A little red dot lights up beside the living room button. *"Ryan?" Click.*

I need to answer. I pull off the shirt and climb over my bed to the intercom. I push the button. "Yeah?"

She wants to know what took me so long. I tell her I was sleeping. She says dinner's ready.

I stuff the altered shirt under my mattress.

I wait for a lonely moment, for the space between the sixth and seventh drinks when Todd thinks of me and texts. When a message doesn't come by eleven, I shut my eyes and wait for sleep. It comes in stutters. I want feature-length dreams and I barely get the trailers. I reach for the phone each time and nothing.

I know what he's doing. The summer before we met, there was Justin. I visited this chat room for years. I never had the guts to meet anyone off it. Instead, I existed on the fringes, peering into this world that felt so foreign but, at the same time, so familiar. These guys were just like me, and they were everywhere. Justin was a regular. I was afraid someone would figure out who I was, so I never used the same username twice. Every time Justin and I spoke, he met someone different. Ashton from Marrickville. Freddie from St. Ives. He told the same introductory anecdotes, and every time, I wanted to learn that little bit more. I committed to a regular username one night. I introduced myself as Ryan from Bondi-ish. We traded numbers. He asked to meet on Town Hall steps one afternoon. I agreed. I watched him from across the street. He paced in figure eights. He checked his phone. He rang. I freaked. I faded away. I didn't message him, and when he messaged me, I didn't write back. He got the hint and faded too.

The longer the message goes unanswered, the more certain of it I feel: Todd's fading. There's a heaviness in my heart. It's tearing stitch by stitch. If this is the end, I want the worst of it in an instant. I want a clean break.

I dial his number.

The world is still. There's a dial tone in the dark. He picks up. "Hello?"

I swallow hard. "Did I wake you?"

"No, I just got home." His voice is flat. "You're up late."

"You didn't reply."

He's quiet and I know what's coming. I clench my free hand. I'm ready.

"I want to wait for you. I tell myself it doesn't matter how long, that I'll be happy so long as I'm with you—" Todd's voice shakes "—and then I wonder what you're waiting for. To suddenly like girls? To meet a better guy? The truth is, I'm not enough to make you sure."

"That's…" I want to tell him that he's wrong, but he isn't.

"I think you need to find someone who's as…not ready as you are."

My eyes begin to water. I blink, as if that will stop them. "Todd."

"I really love you, Italy." It crashes over me and I can't say anything back. The call ends.

———————

The Squad has this mantra: TITF. Take it too far. It's for when we catch ourselves slacking or getting distracted. When we TITF, we eat, sleep and breathe swimming. There's nothing else. We live for the pool, for the victory.

It's all I have left. After Isaac, after Todd. The life I built in twenty-four seconds is gone, but I can build a better one in twenty-three.

I'm first to Squad and last to leave. I swim more laps than the week before. I eat more, push harder, race faster.

And when I tell Mom I'm going for a jog, there's nothing else. I TITF.

The remainder of the quarter disappears behind toppling goals. I keep it up through Easter break. Come second quarter, the Squad splinters. Only the guys with the best times in their age groups have to prep for the All Schools competition. The others join rugby and soccer teams for the winter.

I get my own lane. There's nothing else. First period is always half over by the time I get there. I apologize. "Squad went long." I set myself up in a spare seat, rest my head on my hand and blink at the whiteboard, my eyelids heavy, until the xylophone.

Every day.

Every—

"Ryan!" Mr. Butler's voice wrenches me out of my nap. There's a tiny kid with a parachute for a shirt standing at the door. "Sorry to disturb you, but Ms. Thomson would like to see you in her office."

I cock my head to one side. That's weird. Mom's never sent a kid on office duty to pull me out of class before. It's just asking for—

"*Ooh*, Mama's boy."

That. It's asking for that.

"Shut up, Omar." On his way to the front of the class, Mr. Butler tells me to take my things.

As soon as I'm out, I check my phone. There's no message from Mom. I walk faster. The messenger scurries to keep up. Elise is leaving the staff room as we get there. I catch the door, slip inside and cross the room. Mom's at her desk. Someone's in there with her. He turns to me. Miles. I didn't even notice he wasn't in Modern History.

Mom tells me to close the door. I dump my bag against it and take the vacant seat beside Miles. I ask, "What's up?"

There's a quiet moment before Mom snaps, "Are you fucking stupid?"

I almost fall off my chair. Miles doesn't flinch.

Mom glances into the adjoining staff room and lowers her voice. "I am the head of fucking English. Do you have any idea how bad it looks if…?" She scrunches her face and balls her left hand into a trembling fist.

"What's happening?" I ask. Miles's expression is blank. There are no answers there. I look back to Mom.

"Oh, all right. That's how you're playing it?"

I'm worried an honest answer will unleash the Kraken. "Yes?"

No Kraken. Mom raises both eyebrows, adjusts her bracelets and prepares a narration. "I'm inputting grades last night, and something strikes me as really strange. You're familiar with Michael Wilson?"

I nod. I'm familiar with Mike. I know he has loaded parents and will never have to lift a finger in his life. His dad works in textiles. No clue what that means, but the Wilsons have yachts. Plural.

"He's in one of our midrange classes. For the latest take-home, he scored nineteen out of twenty. That's better than most of our top kids. I check the spreadsheet. In the exam last term, he scored twelve. Even accounting for nerves, that's a huge increase in performance. It doesn't seem right. At first, I think he's been marked too easily in the latest task. I look over it. Nope, it's definitely a top-tier response." Mom shifts in her seat. "There are two things I need to deal with as a head. One, is he in the right class? Are there adjustments that need to be made? Two, what's causing his weaker performance under exam conditions? Is it anxiety? Does he need the text in front of him in order to do well? How can we best support him? So I call him in first thing this morning, and you know what he tells me? He doesn't get anxious, no, he just doesn't do the take-homes. He pays for them."

"Oh?" I still don't know what any of this has to do with me.

Mom's staring. "He pays you, Ryan, you dipshit."

"What?"

"You're going to make me walk you through it? Really?"

"Really. I am so lost right now."

"Don't even," she barks. "Not much gets past me. There's an address he emails his tasks to. He waits a week. He's told to come to the aquatic-center change room before school. Under your bag, there's an envelope with his completed essay inside. He takes it and leaves you a fifty."

"This makes no sense," I try.

"I know," Mom says. "I can spot your writing a mile off, and what he's submitted isn't yours."

Ouch.

"And then Michael says he's only done the change-room exchange three times. Two bits of homework and the assessment task. Before that, he used to meet up with Isaac. I look at Isaac's marks and they're even worse, so I think, who do you both have in common?"

She smiles at Miles and it dawns on me. The red pouch of fifties. That's what Miles and Isaac were doing. They were selling essays. That's what Miles was so desperate to hide.

Wait, why isn't he freaking out? He's sitting there, cool and calm.

"I got ahold of Miles's take-home." Mom taps the two essays out on the table between us. "As you can see, whole sentences appear to have jumped from Miles's work to Michael's. I've highlighted these photocopies."

"I see that."

He sold his own work to other kids. Isaac was his front man. That's why he kept the money in his locker. And when Isaac died, Miles needed a new cover. Me. He's taking me down with him.

"Mom, I—"

"Don't 'Mom' me, Ryan. It's clear as day what you and Miles have done." She starts up again. "Are you an idiot? Do you understand how bad this is? My son and his friends are selling black-market essays under my nose."

I wait for Miles to jump in with, "Oh, we are not actually friends." He doesn't.

"This little business stops right now," she says.

Miles speaks up. "It is over."

"I'm between a rock and a hard place. I have grades that I know are compromised, but my hands are tied. I can't get anyone who purchased essays in trouble without implicating you both and diminishing my standing in the process, so thanks for lobbing this shitful ethical Molotov cocktail at me. They could fire me, you know that?"

"Sorry, miss," Miles says.

"You're both lucky the grader has shit for brains and didn't notice," she says. "But if another grade irregularity comes out of the woodwork and I'm not the one who catches it, so help you God." She clears her throat and scrunches the photocopies into a giant paper ball. "Go back to class."

I've had my ass handed to me and I haven't done anything wrong. "Mom—"

Her eyes flare, like she's trying to tell me more than "Look how wide I can open my eyes!"

"I truly—"

"Class, Ryan."

I don't need to be told a third time. I flee Mom's office and the staff room. The door clicks shut and Miles doubles over, laughing.

"Dude, what the hell?" I ask.

He laughs right through it. I should feel mad. I'm trying to. He sold me out.

He leans back and inhales deeply. He's close to tears. "That was so…" He loses it again. He wheezes through an impression of Mom, expletives and all.

"This isn't funny." I harden my jaw to keep from cracking up.

"Well, if you took yourself out of it and looked at it objectively, you would see it was hilarious." Miles exhales deeply. "If it did not involve you—"

"Getting into shit," I finish for him, but I crack up halfway through, so I say it like "shi-ha-ha-ha-hat."

"Why am I laughing?" I'm asking myself more than

him. It makes no sense. He sold me out. But it feels good
to laugh. It's been so long since…

"The Molotov-cocktail bit was beyond," Miles says.

I picture Mom blowing up and rediscover my indig-
nation. "You could have sold the essays anonymously,
but you made it seem like I did it. You threw me under
the bus."

"Relax. I knew she would not do anything if she knew
you were in on it," Miles says. "So I threw you in front of
the bus knowing full well that the bus would stop when
it saw you." He shrugs. "That is different."

The xylophone goes off over the PA.

"Right," he says. "I have class."

He starts in the opposite direction.

"What? No."

He turns back.

"You don't get to use me as a lifeline and then just…"

Miles reaches into his back pocket. His wallet. "What
do you want, then?" he asks. "A cut?"

"No, it's…" It's not about the money. I don't know.
Isaac's gone. Todd's gone. All I do is swim; all I have is
my own lane. I want more. I want to talk to someone.
"Tell me what you do at lunch."

No one uses the computer lab anymore, not since Barton let us bring our own laptops. Back in seventh grade,
we'd be lucky to get a seat at lunch. Now the room's a
cemetery.

Miles is at a computer in the corner. I say, "Hey."

He swivels around. "Hello."

I really should've prepared talking points. I look around. "I remember this room feeling so much bigger."

He nods slowly. "I know, right?"

I sneak a look past him, at his computer. He has an article open.

"Is that what you do all lunch?" I ask. "Read the news?"

"No." He points a remote up at the projector hanging from the ceiling. It shines a blue square onto the wall. "It takes a while to boot up."

"I remember."

Miles minimizes the browser and starts navigating through folders. I sit down on the chair beside his and wait for the blue square on the wall to fill. Miles counts down from five. He points instead of "Zero," and on cue, the blue square is replaced by Isaac from the shoulders up, projected against the wall. He scratches his cheek with his thumbnail and asks, "Are we good to go?" His voice fills the room, amplified by the speakers mounted in its corners.

In two months, he's faded to an outline of vague features, a crooked smile and a mess of ginger hair. But this is so…vivid. I breathe in chunks.

"The projector allows for the cinema experience," Miles says.

He made a short film for English last year. He asked Isaac to help, and Isaac asked us. He must have a ton of unused footage.

"What am I supposed to say?" Isaac asks.

Miles's recorded voice answers, "Whatever. I will mute the audio and split the screen and show what you are supposed to be describing."

"Okay, so anything?" There's mischief in his eyes. "Boobs, tits, ass, dick, fart."

"People will figure out what you are saying."

"But you said, 'Whatever.'"

"Within reason."

"You didn't say that."

"Isaac."

He cackles and I feel a chill. "Shit, I'm getting goose bumps." I point to the raised spots on my arm. "It's like he's here."

"Yeah," Miles mutters.

"How much footage is there?" I ask.

"All up? Twenty-one hours."

"How much is Isaac?"

"Eight, nine maybe."

"That's a lot."

Miles points to the wall. On cue, Isaac asks, "Can you turn the screen thingy around so I can see how I look?"

Miles knows it by heart.

"You look fine," his disembodied voice replies.

"But I wanna see," Isaac pleads.

Behind the camera, Miles sighs. Beside me, Miles rolls his eyes.

The camera rocks slightly. "I have turned the view-finder to face Isaac," the Miles beside me explains.

"No, I get it."

Isaac stares a little to one side. "Damn I'm pretty," he says. "I feel genuinely bad for people who have to try to look this good." He squints. "Wait, does my hair look gray or is that just my shitty eyes?"

I laugh. He was always going on about his shitty eyes.

Miles mouths, "You done?" in time with his recorded voice.

"Don't pressure me," Isaac says. "I can't work under these conditions. I'm color-blind."

"That should not impact your ability to do a simple reading."

Isaac's eyes are wild. "Discrimination!"

I shake my head. "What a jackass."

"The biggest," Miles says.

The footage ends, frozen on the final frame. I watch Miles watch the screen, Isaac frozen in time and larger than life. We've never had much in common, but we have this.

"It is like when a TV show is on for a while and the main actor leaves to pursue a movie career, the others have to fill the void and keep it going," he says eventually. "People tune in at first, out of curiosity, but it is never the same and definitely never as good. New episodes keep coming, but the viewership dwindles. People stop caring about it, they find something new, but while everyone else can change the channel, the actors cannot. They are contractually obliged to live out the season, stuck there even though they know their best episodes are behind them."

He searches my face for any kind of confirmation that

we're on the same shitty TV show. Are we? Nothing feels like how it used to, I get that. But my show started before Isaac, and I have to believe it can work without him.

"You must see yourself as more than a bit player in someone else's story, though."

"Must I?" Miles asks. "You might—you have swimming and all that—but who would really watch a show about the kid with good grades?"

I slide onto the front edge of my seat and wait for words. "Miles, you're smart, but you're also devious and you don't really consider how your choices affect other people. You're either going to be one of those billionaire media moguls or a very successful white-collar criminal."

"Thanks…I think."

"I would binge-watch the hell out of your show. Mostly because in small doses, you terrify and confuse me."

He forces a laugh. "So funny."

A heavy silence hangs between us. He sniffs.

"If you're unhappy with your show, let me in. Let me help make it better."

"Like as a guest star?"

"With an eye to becoming a series regular if it feels right. What do you say?"

I hold out my hand. He leaves me hanging.

"Shake my hand."

"I am not shaking your hand."

"Shake it."

He shakes it. It's brief but a big deal.

"I am just impressed you know what a series regular is," he says.

"Shut up."

———

I dream of Isaac. He sits opposite me and asks, "What am I supposed to say?"

———

I try the passenger door, but at some point between home and school, Mom locked me in. Squad starts in five minutes, but she doesn't care. She pulls the key from the ignition and twists her whole body to better face me. After almost a day of radio silence, here it comes. The parenting.

"I understand why you did it," she tells me, sounding much calmer than she had in her office yesterday.

"You do?"

"Yes. Isaac helped Miles, and you just did what he would have done," she says. "It's noble, but let's face it, there were times when Isaac wasn't exactly the greatest role model."

I don't say anything. It's easier than having to explain that Miles is a Machiavellian nightmare.

"Fill his absence, but do it on your terms," she continues. "Yes, you should be there for Miles, but you don't have to be Isaac. Don't compromise who you are. Okay?"

"Okay."

"You're an idiot, but you have a good heart and I love you for it."

The car doors unlock. I lunge for the handle, stop and look back. "I'm sorry."

She furrows her brow. "Go swim."

I climb out and swing my bags over my shoulders. There's something post–zombie apocalypse about the underground parking garage this early in the morning. Of the two hundred spots, only two others are taken. There's Mr. Watkins's depressing secondhand convertible and the beat-up van the drama department uses to transport props.

I whistle four short bursts. The sound bounces around the empty space. I start rapping a verse—

"No!" Mom barks. The echoes concur.

When I get there, Mr. Watkins's already stalking the edge of the pool, shouting instructions at the guys doing laps. I duck into the change room.

Dave and Peanut are having a tiff. Back in, like, seventh and eighth grade, an argument was an event. It was exciting. We thought there was a chance someone might throw a punch. We know better now. They always fizzle out to nothing, just two guys not knowing it's over, fatigued and tripping over their testosterone-fueled words but too proud to acknowledge they've stopped making sense.

I dump my stuff to one side and tune it out. I start peeling off my tracksuit top and—

"Yeah, have a cry, you homo."

My zipper catches. It's like the word activates some kind of fight-or-flight response in me. My heart pumps hard.

I didn't know Peanut was gay...

"Stop calling me that," he says.

I continue to undress, like I don't find their exchange interesting in the slightest.

"And if I don't?" Dave goads. "Gonna hit me? Go on."

Dave's a barrel of knotted muscles. Peanut's an arrow. He has some strength in him, but it's not a fight he can win. He clenches a small, trembling fist all the same. He thinks about it. That's his downfall. Before he takes a swing, Dave shoves him back. He crumbles down on the bench beside his bags. Dave isn't the sort of guy to think before he acts.

"Thought so. Homo." Dave saunters toward the door. On his way past, his eyes meet mine and I worry they'll betray me. He smiles. "Oh, hey, man."

He doesn't think I'm gay. I'm relieved.

Peanut hunches over, defeated. He stares at the floor between his feet and this guilt creeps over me. I should have stepped in. I should have called Dave out. I should have had the guts to stop him.

Peanut erupts. He swings his sports bag against the wall with a frustrated grunt.

He looks back to the floor and my guilt intensifies.

I step forward and stretch out a sympathetic "Heeeeeeey."

He doesn't respond, so I ask how he is.

"It's bullshit," he spits.

I want to placate him but he's right. It is bullshit.

"I totally get it," I say.

Peanut squints up at me. "What would you know?"

Of course. I forgot I'm speaking through a closet door.

In his eyes, I'm straight. I've spent so long keeping hidden I've become an expert liar. In an instant, my mind manufactures a gay cousin, Peanut's age—someone I can speak through.

"See, I have this…" I stop myself.

Peanut feels the same way I do. Why am I hiding behind a fabricated cousin? I can speak as myself and make his world a little less dark.

"I'm gay." I laugh, a short release of pressure. "What would I know? You want to be who you are, but you've been taught all the words for it are insults. You've probably used them yourself. *Homo, fag, gay.* You want to be honest, but you're scared that all they'll think when they see you are the insults. So you say nothing, like that'll solve it. But instead of the bullshit being around you, it seeps inside you. It becomes heavy and it grows, and you can't hide it from yourself. And it tortures you. I know because it tortures me." I exhale.

Peanut blinks. "Dude, I'm not gay."

"What?"

He curls his lip. "It's my last name. Caroline. They always give me shit for it."

My heart skips a beat.

"You're a homo?" he asks.

My mind blurs, like someone's spilled its thoughts on a blank canvas and smeared them all together. The more I try to focus, the less I can make out. And then, clarity. My thoughts twist into a face under a mess of ginger hair.

I need Isaac.

———

The computer lab is locked. I lean against the door and take a shallow breath. There's no guarantee that Miles even comes before school, but I wait anyway.

As time creeps by, I feel my secret spread. I see Peanut on the rope telling the first guy that stops at the wall, "Ryan's gay." I imagine it bouncing from person to person, around the school like it's an echo in a post-apocalyptic parking garage. Only inverted. Instead of getting softer with each repetition, it gets louder.

Miles arrives at half past seven. He's surprised to see me. "Oh, hello."

"I tried—" I clear my throat. "It's locked."

Miles raises an eyebrow. "No, it is not." He takes a key from his pocket and twists it in the lock. The door opens. "See?"

"Whose—?"

"Do not ask."

I follow him inside. He walks to his computer, leans over the keyboard and types his log-in details. He then points the remote up at the projector and the blue square lights the room.

I pull up a chair and suddenly fear I'm intruding. "You don't mind me being here, do you?" I ask.

Without turning from the screen, Miles says, "No." He clicks deeper into the folder hierarchy until he gets to a grid of video files. He scrolls through them until one thumbnail catches his eye. "Ah!" He waits for the

screen to project on the wall before he selects the clip.
"You will like this one."

Isaac and I stand in the school courtyard. The wind
is whipping at our hair and lashing at the microphone.
It bursts from the speakers. Off camera, Miles shouts,
"Action!"

There's a delay between the "Action!" and the acting.
I become rigid and very unsure of what to do with my
hands. After attempting some kind of karate stance, I
place them on my waist and leave them there. Seriously,
it's like I'm frozen in a department-store menswear catalog. Isaac's transformation is more graceful. He assumes
his character. Each of his movements is natural, but he's
not moving like he naturally would have. He's an actor.

"I know what you did," I recite. My neck is so straight.

Isaac's fluid. "Really? What do you—? Oh!" He breaks
and looks behind the camera, a little to the left. "Did
Ryan tell you about last night?"

Miles doesn't sound impressed. "Isaac, we do not have
much time."

"I'll be quick," he insists. "Ryan went on a date."

I sit up straighter. I remember this. It's the day after
Todd and I saw our first movie together. Isaac knows.
And I'm thinking he's about to tell Miles…

"What is her name?" Miles asks.

Isaac gives me a chance to correct him. When I don't,
he covers for me. "Her name's Dot."

"Dot?" Miles asks. "That is retro."

Isaac's grinning. He's so proud of himself for thinking
of Todd backward.

Miles asks if I am going to see her again, and I'm reluctant to answer. Eventually, I tell him I'm not sure.

"Yes, he is," Isaac says, before he looks to me. "You are."

He wants me to give Todd a proper shot. He won't let me toss it away because we're both dudes. I nod and restrain a smirk.

"Right. We are wasting battery," Miles says. "Get in position."

I glue my hands to my waist again, and as he relaxes into his character, Isaac winks.

"And, action!"

Sitting in the lab, I wipe my eyes with two fingers. They're wet. I look to Miles. I can almost feel Isaac urging me on. "Miles?"

He turns from the wall. *"Hmm?"*

I hesitate. I wonder how long I have left, how long it takes for the Olympic hopeful to turn into the Olympic homo. Peanut's still doing laps. It won't get out for another hour at least.

One more hour. I want to savor it.

"I should change before a teacher sees I'm only wearing a tracksuit over my Speedo and flips their shit," I say.

"Are you not training this morning?"

I shrug. "Don't need to."

I'm Ryan Patrick Thomson, Olympic hopeful.

———

I go to the spot that's ours. There's no one sitting there. A little rain and the courtyard's deserted, save for the rugby faithful. They jog in one line, grunting team-talk as they pass the ball.

I wipe the table sort of dry with my sleeve and sit up on it, feet on the bench. I exhale.

I've been so careful for so long, and this is how it happens. I open up to someone, thinking it'll help him, and he's not even gay. It's his fucking name. There's a part of me that knows it's funny, only the rest of me isn't quite ready to laugh about it yet.

I rest my hands beside me. One lands on a loose flake of green paint. Curious, I pick at it, until there's enough to pinch and peel back to reveal the wood underneath.

"Jeez, who died?" someone asks.

I look up. Harley's standing with one hand in his blazer pocket, the other wrapped around an impossibly large coffee cup. He takes a sip.

"I'm back."

THE REBEL

THE WEATHER'S TURNED. THE SUN'S PISSED OFF
and the wind's picked up. That's my cue. I toss back the
dregs and drop the empty bottle. It clinks against the
others. I sit forward in the deck chair. "Okay, I'm calling it."

Zac looks wounded. Well, as wounded as he can look
sitting on a bucket in a neon safety vest and board shorts.
"Already?"

I stand up and have to steady myself. Shouldn't of had
that last one.

"Yeah, dinner curfew. Besides, school tomorrow. Better sober up for all that learning."

Zac burps. "Harley, we're sober." He reaches for the
bourbon he stole from his dad's cabinet and messily tops
off a Mom of the Year mug. "*I'm* sober, anyway." He starts
slurring the alphabet backward to prove it. "Z, Y, X…"

"I was kidding. I legit don't care."

"*Z, Y, X,*" he repeats forcefully. I let him carry on.

There's a rough patch from O to H, but he gets to A in the end. Proud, he tilts the bottle at me.

I shake my head. "Seriously, dude, I gotta—"

"For the road," he insists.

"Already called it."

"Heads up!" It isn't much of a warning. The rugby ball smacks the deck chair and bounces toward the fence. "Sorry," Omar adds.

"Hey." Zac turns on the bucket, which is difficult to do. "That's not cool." There's spillage when he waves his mug.

Omar's uneasy. "Almost hitting Harley?" he asks.

"Sports," Zac spits.

Marty found the ball behind the shed, Ex suggested they play and Omar told them to give him a sec to finish his drink. That was hours ago. They've tossed the ball around Zac's yard since.

"Dude, you're burned as fuck," Marty says.

"Can't be." Zac points at the yellow streaked across his cheeks. "I'm wearing sunscreen."

He watches them until Ex says he doesn't see the harm in one more. They head to the cooler.

"That's right," Zac mumbles into his mug. The back of his neck is bright red.

"You are pretty burned," I tell him.

"Oh, I know."

I laugh. It's all I can do sometimes. "You're good for tomorrow, yeah?"

Zac racks his brain. When it comes up blank, he squints at me. "Remind me…"

"Coffee with Jacs."

"Ah." He watches the others nurse their brews. "Should be fine. Don't see tonight lasting much longer."

The boardinghouse backs onto Woods Lane. There's a couple of bins, a car without a bumper and nothing else. No one has any real reason to be here, unless they've missed curfew. I wheel a recycling bin to the brick fence, climb up and over. I drop into the courtyard and hiccup. Tastes like spew.

"Sexy," I mutter.

Everyone's in the dining hall for spaghetti night. I sneak into a seat at the junior table. "Pass me the pitcher of water, will you?"

"Where'd you come from?" Hughes asks.

"What? Nowhere. Been here the whole time." He hands over the pitcher and I down three glasses. I scope out the room. Guys are lining up at the buffet for seconds. I need a plate. Hughes clears the last bit of sauce from his. "You done with that?" I ask.

He shrugs. "Pretty much."

I inhale my dinner and take the water pitcher to bed with me.

I hop out of the shower, towel gripped around my waist. Water's running full blast in the five other stalls. I walk around the corner.

"That's halfway!" The door's open just enough for Collins's voice to carry through from the hall. "This is the time to start using soap if you haven't already."

Guys bitch about the six-minute limit, but it's easy to cover the essentials in two. I use the remaining time for selfies. I aim my phone at the huge mirror and twist to show off the design down my right side. I have to draw my tats till I'm old enough to get one for real or I can afford the flight to wherever they won't give a shit about my age. This one's starting to fade already. I take two photos, apply a filter to the best one and send it to Jacs.

JACS
Gross. I'm eating.

ME
I have to be shirtless to show the tat.

JACS
There's a diff between shirtless and wearing only a towel. I can see outlines.
What's it meant to be?

ME
The outlines? Well...

JACS
THE TAT. OH GOD. THE TAT.

"Two minutes," Collins calls.
"Already?" Fuzz asks from his stall.

"Yes. You're not that dirty."

"Oh, he's pretty brown, sir," Hughes adds. The other guys laugh.

"That's kitchen for a week, Mark."

Hughes protests. "But—"

"I can count to two."

"It wasn't racist, sir. He even jokes about it."

"Would you rather three weeks on kitchen duty?"

Hughes goes quiet. "No, sir," he says.

"Great. One minute."

I start to dress. The tat disappears behind my white shirt.

JACS

Is it a tree?

ME

Nah, just the leaves.

JACS

Too hard to draw branches?

ME

No tree roots hold me down.

JACS

Deep. You should get that done across your shoulders in calligraphy.

ME

For real?

JACS
No.
Nothing in calligraphy.
Ever.

I met Jacs my second night in Sydney. The boarding-house has these dinners with Barton's sister school, Our Sacred Something of the Holy Whatever. Jacs boards there. Good friends need to like the same movies and hate the same people. Jacs quoted Quentin Tarantino and seemed to hate most people. So, yeah, it worked.

JACS
How long will you be?

ME
Fifteen. Depends.

JACS
On what?

Breakfast, the line at the coffee shop, the walk to Hyde Park. To fit in coffee, the rest of my morning has to happen at the speed of light.

I can feel Olive and Jo watching me from the kitchen as I shovel scrambled eggs into a napkin. They're paid to feed us; the motherly disapproval comes free of charge.

"I'm taking it to go," I explain.

Jo wishes me luck. I don't think I need it. I leave. I manage to have two bites before the napkin sags forward and the egg tumbles onto the pavement.

"Shit."

JACS

Sophie saw your pic.

ME

She saw it?

JACS

I showed her.

"Order for Harley?" the barista calls.

I look up. There's a tray of three drinks by the coffee machine.

ME

What's the verdict?

JACS

She thinks you look Spanish.

Irish-Dutch-Lithuanian-German-Inuit... With that many hyphens, you come out looking some kind of Spanish.

ME

And the tat?

JACS

She approves.

I think it's a winner, Scott.

My folks didn't name me. I was hours old when they wrote options on a whole bunch of Post-its, covered my body with them and waited for me to name myself. I touched *Scott* first and they went with that. People just call me Harley, unless they're Jacs. She calls me whatever she wants.

JACS

Seriously, ETA?

ME

I'm right in front of you.

Jacs is waiting on the edge of the Archibald Fountain. She looks up from her phone.

"Hey." I hold out the tray.

She takes her latte. "Your fly's undone."

"It's not." I check my zipper. It's all the way up.

Jacs chews on a smile. "Never gets old," she says.

"Any sign of Zac?" I ask.

She shakes her head.

I shoot him a text. We sip our drinks. I slouch forward. She taps her feet. We sip our drinks.

"We probably shouldn't send, like, a hundred texts right before we catch up," Jacs says.

"True."

She exhales and sits back. She pulls on the elastic band around her wrist, and her eyes drift to the drink with Zac written on the lid. "What did he order?" she asks.

She grabs it and takes a sip. "Oh, gross." That doesn't stop her sipping some more.

I check my phone. Zac hasn't texted. He's probably asleep. Trust him to play hooky and not tell anyone.

"He was pretty wrecked yesterday," I explain.

"Mm." Jacs hops up.

"Where are you going?"

She raises an eyebrow. "School. You know, that thing we do every day?"

"He could still show."

Jacs sighs. "But then he'd know I waited." She walks backward and two suits split up to dodge her. She points at me. "Make better friends, Scott Harley."

At Barton, they're always going on and on about learning opportunities. Evans pulls me out of class to talk about them.

We have a special relationship, the two of us. She hauls me in every February, tells me it's my year. Then I get results back that aren't too hot, or I grow my hair out past what's acceptable, or I laugh at something legit hilarious like a kid tripping down the stairs, and I'm back and she's all like, "Scott, I thought we said this was your year..."

Thing is, when she hauls me in, I usually know why. Cuz I write an acrostic poem instead of an essay in an English exam, cuz I refuse to get a haircut on religious grounds, cuz four students and a staff member say they saw me push a Twelvie down the stairs.

It hasn't exactly been the Year of Harley so far, but

I'm doing all right. I don't write sarcastic poems when I don't know the answer, I don't insist I'm Rastafarian, and I don't elbow younger kids who get in my way.

So hell if I know why I'm here.

Or why *he's* here.

Miles sits bolt upright at the other end of the waiting room. He's reading the cookbook Barton published. Three hundred glossy, full-color pages celebrating the school's proud traditions, mixing inspiring stories with delicious recipes from students, their families and staff. Basically, someone in Marketing wanted Barton to seem *more* up its own ass.

"Hey."

Miles doesn't look up.

"Hey."

He looks up. His lips are all attitude like he's annoyed I've interrupted a scone recipe.

"What are you in for? Here to ask Evans for a Time-Turner?"

His mouth drops open. "Wow, you can read?"

"Nah, saw the movie."

He rolls his eyes. "Of course you did."

"For real, though, why are you here?" I ask.

"Mrs. Evans sent for me."

"You're busted."

His face whitens, and he was practically albino to start with.

"I am not...*busted.*"

I nod. "You're busted."

Thommo comes in from the hallway. "Yeah, you're a goner," he adds. He sinks into a seat near me.

"You too?" I ask.

"Apparently. What did we do?" Thommo asks.

"You and me? No clue. He's just after a Time-Turner."

Miles snaps the cookbook shut. "Will you...*stop* saying that?"

"*Oof,*" Thommo says. "Someone's on edge."

I don't see why. They'll be fine. Thommo's untouchable cuz he's the top swimmer and his mom works here, and Miles is Teflon. Nothing sticks to him. If Thommo's Barton's best, Miles is its brightest. Perfect record, perfect grades and glasses that are more supervictim than supervillain.

But me? I give off major supervillain vibes. Whatever we've done, it's my fault. I've been at Barton long enough to know that.

Evans will probably give me another after-school detention that makes no sense cuz I'm a boarder and my life is one long after-school detention anyway.

"What do you think he has done?" Miles asks.

"Who?" Thommo asks.

"Isaac." He says it like it's obvious.

"What makes you think he's done something?" I ask.

Miles licks his chapped bottom lip. "Well, I have not done anything. Have you?"

"Maybe?"

It's not the answer he wants. He turns to Thommo.

"No."

"And all three of us? At the same time? No—" Miles

shakes his head "—this is about Isaac. He is our common denominator."

He's obviously never been called to see Evans before.

"Why would we be pulled out of class if he's done something wrong?" I ask. "That makes no sense."

Miles goes to speak but then shuts his mouth. Before I can gloat, Evans opens her office door. "Could you come inside, boys?" she asks.

Miles rises, Thommo springs up and I stay put. It's weird. The only "could you" I usually hear from Evans comes before "shut up." She's a woman of short directives. "Go to class." "Clean yourself up." "Come inside."

"Could you" is weird.

***

My head's scrambled. Something went down after I left last night—I need to know what. I duck out of the chapel while Evans dismisses everyone by rows. I wait down the hall. Omar's out first. He's a head taller than everyone else. He sees me and hurries over. He asks if he needs a lawyer.

"That's your first thought? Zac is dead, you dipshit. What the fuck happened after I left?"

"Nothing. Isaac went home."

"Went home? You were already at home. Where did you go?"

Omar stumbles over his words. Lanky spaghetti fuck can't string a sentence together when it counts. Marty and Ex swoop in to save him.

"Where were you?" I ask.

"We have to say something." I can hear Ex's heartbeat in his voice. "We were there. We have to."

I try to keep calm. "Right. Walk me through it."

"I don't know," Ex continues. "We thought he—"

Marty talks over him. "Isaac's parents were coming back, so we went down to the motorboat club. There was no one else there. We set up on the pier, but he wanted to sneak onto the boats. We just chilled and let him do whatever. He climbed one that had a cabin and dove off."

Shit. That's when he hit his head…

"He came back soaked," Omar adds.

I exhale.

"He went home cuz he was drenched," Ex says.

"And that's it, right?" Omar asks.

"No." Marty remembers something. "First he wanted to do it again, remember? He asked us to have a go. We wouldn't. He disappeared and… I just figured he caved, went home without saying anything. A good old Irish goodbye."

"He was wasted."

"More than drunk."

"Shit," I mutter. "We're screwed."

"Not *we*, though, right?" Omar looks me dead on. "You're the one who…" He trails off.

I know what he's thinking, and the others don't disagree with him. Marty turned and gave me this look in the chapel. It was written on his face.

"You're gonna blame me?" I ask. "I wasn't there."

"But you…you know."

I know a guy. He's not seedy or anything—he's a regular guy, only resourceful. If there's something we're after, he can probably get it. I don't widely advertise. It's a service for friends, and it's not as if I make a mint from it. I just skim a bit from the top, enough for a coffee.

"This isn't my fault," I insist.

"Isn't it?" Marty asks.

———

There's a liquor store near Barton. I find a half-drunk guy in the McDonald's across the street and give him enough for a six-pack. He comes out with three bottles. There's no use challenging him. He's doing me the favor.

Three beers is barely enough for a buzz. Stretch them over a three-hour train ride down the coast and they're pointless. I can still hear Marty in my head telling me it's my fault. I can still remember Zac resting his elbow on my shoulder, leaning his weight on me and asking, "Think your guy can get us more?"

The train car rocks. I take a swig.

———

Dad was born in Gerringong. He says he'll die here.

He won't have to wait long if he keeps hiding the spare key under a potted plant out front. I let myself in. The place smells like a middle-aged bachelor. There are clothes piled in random places.

I find two six-packs in the fridge, but I figure Dad's

on top of how many he has and how long they'll last him. I try the pantry. There's a stash of red wine bottles collecting dust. Mom's leftovers. I grab one by the neck.

A cupboard door slams. A drawer opens. There's the clash of silverware. I push up off the sofa. It's pitch-black outside. Dad's a broad-shouldered shadow in the blinding light.

"Morning, petal," he says.

I'm squinting. "It isn't, is it?"

"No."

I swallow hard and taste the vomit mixed with red wine in the back of my throat. Food. I need food. I look around. There's a pizza box on the floor. I stretch out and lift the lid with my toe—no leftovers.

"You wish, bud," Dad says. "You're getting toast. That'll teach you to call before you visit."

"I must've fallen asleep," I croak.

"No shit." He comes around the breakfast bar with a plate and a can of beer. He hands me the plate and keeps the beer. He drops onto the single-seater and splays his knees out.

People say I look like him. Yeah, before the divorce and apocalypse maybe. His salt-and-pepper stubble is less pepper than it was at Christmas, and his face is more cracked.

"You're lucky they called me and not your mother," he says. "For such a fancy place, they don't seem too keen on calling overseas."

"Or they're scared of her."

Dad laughs. "True. Can't imagine she'd like 'em saying they lost you."

I pick up a toast slice. Dad's overdone the Vegemite.

He gulps his beer and smacks his lips. "Running off wasn't that smart. I covered for you, said I told you to come."

"Thanks."

He's looking at his beer can like there's courage at the bottom of it. "How much trouble are you in?"

He knows about Zac.

"I wasn't there." It doesn't really answer his question.

He strums the top edge of his can with his thumb. "And you're…all right?"

There's an anchor tied around my chest.

I shrug. "What's the use if I'm not? Won't change anything."

"Have you told your mother?"

I shake my head. I haven't spoken to Mom much since… Not since Barton. It had been her idea to send me there. She thought a private school in the city would do me good, mold me into a fine young man, all that crap. A lot of good it's done.

"I have to tell her you're here."

I can't stop him, but I try to negotiate. "After I fall asleep?"

He checks the clock and does the conversion in his head. I can tell it's been a while since he called the States. There are cobwebs to clear. He gets there eventually. "You better hit the hay, then."

———

I wake up. My brain's having a fistfight with my skull. I groan and force my eyes open. The room is bright. Instead of traffic and Twelvies, I hear…a lawn mower? It takes me a sec to catch up with my body. I'm in Gerringong. I ran away from Barton. Zac died.

"Fuck." I roll over and check my phone. It doesn't respond to my touch and I remember the battery didn't last the trip down.

I sit up and my brain slams my skull. Red wine. Never again.

I'm still in my school shirt. It's wet, stuck to my chest like another layer of skin. I shed it.

"Dad?" I call.

He doesn't reply.

I cross the hall into blue. Everything in the bathroom is some shade of it. I cram my head into the sink and switch on the tap. I gulp. Water runs out of my mouth and down my left cheek. I pull up and wipe my face with the back of my hand.

"Dad?" I ask again.

Nothing. He must be gone for the day.

I twist a little. I've sweated most of the tat off.

I head back across the hall. Whenever I come back to Gerringong, my room feels smaller. Everything does. I get older and the world shrinks. I open my wardrobe. Nothing in it will fit—it's all from before the move.

I should of planned my escape better, packed a bag or something.

"Good one, Harley," I mutter.

One of my skate posters curls off the wall. On my way past, I press the corner back. The second I remove my finger, the poster folds off the wall worse than before.

Dad's room is at the front of the house. I plug my

phone into the charger by his bed and raid his closet while it boots up. It'll take ages to connect to the network. This street is a black hole.

I settle for tennis shorts and a T-shirt, both spoiled by flecks of paint.

There's an uninterrupted stream of chimes and vibrations. My phone's found the network. Forty-seven notifications. I scroll through the list and stop at Mom.

MOM
Your father called.

Brief, to the point, all while avoiding it. Mom's signature style.

She has a proven track record. She didn't send me away to feel less guilty about leaving; she *wanted to give me a chance at a better life*. She didn't hate living in a small Aussie town; she was *offered a job in Brooklyn*. She didn't fall out of love; she just *didn't think it was fair to stay together*.

She's a bullshit artist.

Whatever. She's back in the States, where she grew up. Dad and I were a detour.

I don't reply. There's no use pretending like we're closer than we are.

I leave my phone to charge and walk up the back. Dad's left a carton of eggs in a pan on the stove with a note: "Explains itself."

Part of me wants to fry the carton and send him the photo, but that'd probably piss him off. I fry three eggs close together so the whites mix. I fold the massive thing over itself and stab it with a fork like an egg Popsicle. I plate it and streak barbecue sauce over the top. Between bites, I dunk my head under the kitchen tap and a chug a liter.

———————

I hover around my phone till it hits 50 percent. That'll do.

I take it out onto the back deck. Now there are sixty-two notifications to clear. Everyone asking where I am, what I know.

My phone goes off in my hand. It's a fresh text.

JACS
Hey.

I scroll back up through the convo, till I recognize the messages from yesterday morning.

JACS
Thanks for coffee. Was good fun.
Thank Zac for his coffee. Wasn't too bad.

JACS
Dude. I just heard.

JACS
DUDE.

JACS
You there?

JACS
Scott... Please, say something.

JACS
Please.

JACS
Hey.

I want to reply but I know I can't. Sydney is done, and the sooner I act like it, the easier this'll be.

I quit the convo and scan the rest of the texts. Five guys send me a link to the same *Herald Daily* news story. I cave and open it.

"Aspiring actor with great potential—we are deeply saddened": Model student from one of Australia's most exclusive schools dies after "hijinks"

PUBLISHED YESTERDAY AT 1:55 PM,
UPDATED TODAY AT 10:57 AM

- Isaac Roberts jumped or fell from a motorboat early Monday morning, sustained head injury

- Drinking and "hijinks" with friends beforehand, police say

- Heartfelt tributes paid to much-loved sixteen-year-old

He *jumped or fell*. My eyes sting. I scroll down until the dot–point summary's gone.

They've used a photo of him at a hipster party, with a collarless shirt buttoned right to the top. It's probably the most formal he's ever looked outside his uniform. Seems smart too—he's wearing glasses. They're just a pair of empty frames, though.

Anyone who knew him will know he was making fun. Everyone else will think how lovely and intelligent he looks.

He was an aspiring actor apparently. First I've heard of it.

I skim the rest of the article.

His body was found five hours after he was last seen… The Barton House community is in mourning… Kathleen Evans, deputy headmistress of the exclusive all-boys inner-city school, said the community's thoughts and prayers are with his family…

There's a photo of the guys on the pier with police. I can make out Ex and Marty. They're holding flowers.

"He was a great guy," close friend Xavier Jones said.

I'm suddenly white-hot. My grip tightens. My hand shakes. "You left him there! You didn't even know he was…" I toss the phone into the yard and chew on my thumbnail.

"*Close friend*, my ass."

———

I dust off a bottle of red. It's a 2010 Shiraz. Hell if I know what that means, but the first mouthful is harsh. The next one's better.

I wipe the soil off the screen and the article scrolls. It stops on a block of text.

"He was an aspiring actor. His talents and great potential were on display when he took part in our pilot young-filmmakers program last year," Mrs. Evans wrote in a letter on the school's website.

I read it again, in case it sounds less like a shameless plug the second time.

It doesn't.

"Hi. I have some questions about an article on your website…" I hold down a burp. It tastes like 2010 Shiraz. "I was wondering if I could speak to the reporter who… Oh… Is there anyone I can talk to? An editor person?… Okay. Well, could I give you my number? Cuz there's this bit where it says…"

I tune in halfway through Channel Seven's new game show and try to make sense of it. Nina from Camberwell's about to answer a question to double her money or some shit, and Dad mutes the TV from the kitchen.

"Hey, what gives?"

"I asked you what you got up to today."

"I sat out on the deck, and now I'm sitting here." I also drank a bottle of 2010 Shiraz. I also spilled some on a pillow. I also walked down the street to toss out an empty bottle of 2010 Shiraz and a pillow.

"Well, that's…" Dad struggles to find a supportive word. He turns back to the burger patties sizzling on the stove.

My phone vibrates. I fish it out from between the sofa cushions.

"What's on the agenda tomorrow?" Dad asks.

JACS

Just tell me you're okay.

"Scott?"

"Hmm?" I drop the phone back between the cushions. "Yeah, I'm okay." Shit. He didn't ask that. "Nothing, I dunno."

Dad doesn't push it.

————

I pop the cap off and hesitate. Zac notices.

"Just do whatever." He's sitting in the tub, holding a chipped Mother's Day mug loaded with bourbon. "Do the lines again. They were cool."

A couple of tats ago, I had horizontal red stripes up my arm. The higher they got, the more they shortened at both ends, but I ran out of arm to make a point.

"No, I want something for here this time." I slap my right side hard enough to leave a palm print.

"Have you thought about flora?"

"Flora?"

"Plants, you dumbass."

"Yeah. I'm gonna draw a fucking flower down my body."

"I don't fucking know." Zac spits a laugh. "*Fuck*'s a funny word. They should let us say it more."

"You say it enough, I'm sure."

"*Mm*." He has a bit to drink. "How about a tree?"

I look at my reflection and imagine one of the massive fig trees from Hyde Park down my side. I dunno. "If someone asks about it, I wanna say it means something, though," I tell him.

"Right. Well, your tree wouldn't have roots."

"Huh?"

His eyes are glassy with fermented wisdom. "You don't strike me as someone who is ever, like, locked into anything. You get me?"

"Sorta?"

"You move, not *with* the wind, but just *in* it." He acts it out with his free hand. "Only draw the leaves, nothing else. Cuz no tree roots can hold you down."

"That's weak."

"It's a metaphor. Miss Pill'd lose her mind if you took your shirt off and showed her."

I shrug. "What chick wouldn't?"

"Boom."

I bounce it back. "Boom."

I press the Sharpie's tip against my skin, then open my eyes. I'm in bed, in Gerringong, miles away from Zac's bathroom. It was a dream. It had felt so real. It *was* real. I don't remember much of Sunday, but I remember that. I was by the sink and he was in the tub.

I push the covers down and stretch my skin so I can see more of the tat. It's faded to a gray whisper.

I kick off the sheets and raid the kitchen's drawer of miscellaneous crap for a Sharpie. I trace over it. I botch a few leaves, but it's mostly as good as it was before.

I add an extra leaf, blown off to the side.

Pill'd go nuts for that shit.

———

Through the fly screen, Dad asks if I'm coming to bed. I'm sitting on the porch. I tell him I'll be a minute. He asks if I want the light on. I say, "I'm good." My eyes are stuck to the final line of the *Herald Daily* article.

Barton House will host the funeral service for Isaac Roberts on Thursday afternoon, with his peers and key members of the school community expected to attend.

Tomorrow.

Instead of shuffling away, Dad opens the door. He sits and waits like he has all the time in the world.

"There was a party on Sunday." I'm talking into my lap. "I left, but the others stayed. They went down to the pier and Zac *jumped or fell* from a boat. That's what the article says. Here."

I pass the phone over to Dad. He scrolls too far. "Motorboat Bikini Babes?" he asks.

"That's the video at the bottom of the page," I say.

"A bit tacky, no?"

"*Jumped or fell* is worse. Did he jump on purpose? Did he jump on purpose but die by accident? Or did he fall? They can't just say he *jumped or fell* and leave it like that."

Dad hands the phone back. "Get them to change it," he says.

"I tried calling but didn't get past the front desk. I gave the lady my number anyway." I turn the cell phone over in my hands. "They got it wrong. He didn't kill himself."

Dad's quiet for a while. "I'm sure he didn't."

"I killed him. Not on purpose, but…I killed him."

"What do you mean?"

On my first night at Barton, Mom tried calling. I was pissed, so I lay on the bed and let her call vibrate out. The phone fell off the side. I went to grab it and noticed the number scratched into the bed's wooden frame… He was a solid contact. He had this new stuff. I wasn't up for it on Sunday, but Zac wanted to give it a go. He must of. The boys noticed he was more than drunk. When people find out what it was, they're gonna ask where he got it…

"I…just encouraged him to do stupid shit."

"That's why you're here?"

I look at him. "Would you stay?"

"It's not your fault."

Easier said.

"What will you do?" Dad asks.

"What would you do?" I ask.

He thinks. It's like he lays out every word he knows and only speaks when he's picked out the right ones, in the right order. "I think," he says, "whatever you need to do, you can't do from here."

———————

There's a train at half past five that gets me to Kogarah before eight. It's a hike from there to Zac's place. There's enough time to chicken out. I don't. I stop in his driveway.

I take a deep breath and pull back my hood.

I'm not going to wait for them to find something in Zac's system. I'm going to tell them everything.

The front door opens and my heart cramps. Zac's sister steps out, her overnight bag on one shoulder. She's startled when she sees me.

"Hey, Isobel." I tried calling her Izzy once. It didn't go down well. She made the face she's making now, all creases.

"Shouldn't you be at school?" she asks.

"Yeah. I… Your parents are home, right?"

She forces a smile. "They're not really seeing people this morning. It's been a busy few days and they just need to get ready for today." She aims her key at the red truck on the street and pushes the button. The hazard lights blink. "I'll tell them you came, though."

On her way past, I ask her how she's doing.

"Honestly?" Isobel turns, annoyed I haven't left. "I've been better, Harley." She squints. "Why are you here?"

My throat is dry. "I—"

"I thought I heard a familiar voice."

Isobel and I look over at the house. Sue's standing at the door, one hand on her hips, the other shielding her eyes.

"Is that you, Harley?" she asks.

It's like Isobel wants me to say "No."

I hesitate. "Yeah?"

"Come on in."

"Actually…uh… Isobel was gonna give me a lift back to the station."

"Yeah, I was."

"Nonsense. Nobody's in a rush," Sue insists.

Isobel massages her temple and surrenders. She locks her truck and starts the walk back. "Come on."

Sue hangs by the door. I keep my head down, but when I get to her, she pulls me into a tight hug. "Thank you for coming."

I've never been inside Zac's house without him. It's like when one of your earphones craps out, and after being so used to stereo, suddenly, you can only hear mono. It feels…off. Sue leads us to the dining table, to Warwick.

"Look who I found outside," she tells her husband.

He shakes my hand firmly. "Harley."

I'm happy to stand, but Sue tells me to sit. "Isobel's friend Zoey brought over muffins—help yourself." She points to the container on the table. "Did you want any-thing to drink?"

"I'm fine, thanks."

"You sure? Just ask if you do." She eases into the seat beside Warwick's. "How are you feeling?"

Guilt burns a course inside me. I did this. And *they're* asking *me* how I am.

"I'm okay—how are you?"

Sue looks to her husband. He chews on a muffin slowly. "We're… It's such a shock, and not quite real yet." She breathes through her nose. "How are the others?"

"The others?"

"Ryan and Miles."

I have no idea. I haven't spoken to them since Mon-day. "Oh, they're…doing okay."

Her face goes soft. "That's a relief."

I force a smile and Sue recognizes something. Her mouth hangs open.

"You smile exactly like him," she says.

It's like the words reach inside me and stop my heart. "Sorry, can I use the bathroom?"

"Sure."

I can't get up fast enough. I shut the bathroom door and breathe out everything that's in me.

I picture my confession, my sentences collapsing into each other cuz I need to get it out: I fucked up and I'm sorry.

Three hours ago I was certain I'd be able to. Now? Not so much. And the window's too small to climb through. I know cuz Zac and I tried. Well, Zac tried.

He got his head and one arm out before announcing he was stuck. I just laughed, you know, for moral support.

If it had been me, he would of told me to suck it up. And it might of worked.

"Suck it up, Harley," I try, thinking it might summon some dormant courage. But it's not the same.

When I get back to the table, I tell Sue I'll have a muffin. I have five. With my mouth full, I don't have to say a word.

———————

I walk the main road back to the station, feeling like a screwup. A three-hour train from Gerringong, and now a three-hour trip back, all so I could choke and not tell them.

Great.

A red truck approaches the curb and slows to my pace. Isobel looks through the passenger window. "How are you getting there today?"

Huh? Oh. The funeral. I didn't think that far. I was going to Zac's, telling the truth and… I didn't think about what'd come next.

Isobel stops and pulls the hand brake. "Let me drive you. Please."

She undoes her seat belt, leans over and opens the passenger door.

I look down at Dad's hoodie and jeans. "I'm not really dressed."

"Like Isaac gives a shit," Isobel says. "Now, if I hang

here, the cops will give me a ticket, and if I leave without you, my mom will kill me. Your move."

———————

Isobel rents a one-bedroom apartment a little closer to
the city. Her sofa tries to eat me when I sit on it. She
apologizes. The place came furnished. She says she won't
be long. I'm welcome to watch TV, if I like. She glances
around. "The remote is…somewhere."

I tell her I'm fine.

After a minute or so, she calls my name.

"Yeah?"

"Can I ask you something?"

I hesitate. "Sure."

"Why did you come by today?" She reappears, bare-
foot and in a black dress. "I mean, you didn't walk all that
way from the station just to eat muffins with us, right?"

There's no use in lying to her. Whatever I couldn't
say at Zac's place, I have to say now. I push myself to the
edge of the cushion so the sofa isn't collapsing in on me.
"I came over to tell your folks—"

"Wait. Let me guess." Isobel licks her bottom lip. "You
were going to tell them you were there on Sunday. Tell
them you always brought booze over."

It hits harder than a punch. My confession hasn't started
yet and it's already backfired. "I was going to apologize."

"That's even better." She collects her hair in one
hand and ties a ponytail. "Make yourself feel good, even
though you've probably fucked their lives. Noble."

There is a fake calmness in her voice, cracking around the edges like she wants to scream at me.

"What else can I do?" I ask.

Isobel comes closer and asks for my phone.

"What?"

She holds out her hand. I give it to her. She swipes the screen and sighs.

"Unlock it?"

I reach over and enter my PIN. The home screen fills in. She goes to Contacts.

"I'm giving you Mom's number," she says. "You're going to call her and take her out for lunch or something. And you're going to sit there while she tells you about her day, which will be shitty, but she'll dress it up so you don't worry about her. And you will tell her about your day. And when she asks about her son, you will share appropriate, heartwarming stories. If you have none, you will make them up."

"Honestly, I think one of the other guys would be better at that."

"Didn't you hear her? You smile exactly like him," Isobel says. "You're Isaac's friends, and he's rubbed off on you. Screw apologies—*that's* what Mom needs."

She hands me my phone and heads back into her room. I stare down at Sue's fresh contact entry.

———

I sink deeper into the pew and glance around. Our entire year is here, along with a couple of teachers and senior staff members whose only job is to look important and wise. They've framed one of his school pictures and stuck it on a bed of flowers. "Flora," Zac'd say.

Looking around, anybody who didn't know Zac would guess he thought the school was hot shit. I guess that's the point, though. When he died, a model student from one of Australia's most exclusive schools took his place.

I check my phone.

MARTY

Hanging with the friends and family, eh?

I'm going incognito in the back row. Well, I thought I was…

ME

Yeah.

MARTY

Where've you been?

ME

Busy.

MARTY

Where though?

Brother Mitchell's talking, so I turn the phone over. He gets us up to sing a hymn and tries to pitch it as something Zac would of wanted. Yeah, this funeral, definitely what he wanted.

I don't sing. I tear my thumbnail with my teeth and catch some dude looking back at me. It's Thommo. He nods slowly and I stare back blankly.

His mom whispers something and he turns around. I sit down before we're told to.

Sue walks up to give a speech and my phone vibrates.

MARTY

We're heading to the pier for our own memorial after this. You in?

I try to focus on what Sue's saying, but my mind drifts to the motorboat club. It might be good to have our own farewell, without the Barton song and dance. And I'd be where Zac last was.

MARTY

Think your guy could score us something special?
You know, for Isaac?

———

The front door closes. Dad drops his keys into the glass ashtray by the door. His boots are heavy on the hardwood floors. Coming closer. The shopping bags rustle. He puts them down on the counter.

"You're here." He sounds surprised.

I'm lying on the sofa, staring past my feet and out the window. "Where else would I be?"

He starts to unpack the shopping. "I just thought, if you were going all that way…"

"Nope."

When he's put everything away, he crumples the empty bags into a ball. "Have you spoken to your mother?"

———

I stare down the last remaining bottle of red in the bottom of the pantry. If I drink it, that's today, but what about tomorrow? And the day after that? I settle for a walk instead. I end up on the strip of shops and cafés leading to the coast. There's a help-wanted sign taped to the window of Bev's Buns. I pop in. The place smells like coffee beans and fresh bread. I ask Bev about the sign, and she asks if I have hospitality experience. I tell her I don't, cuz I know if she had a better option, she'd of taken the sign down by now. She says she doesn't have time to teach someone how to make coffee.

"That's fine. I'll just make bad coffee."

She laughs and asks me when I can start.

On the way out, someone texts.

JACS

Were you there yesterday?

I want to tell her I got a job, but I can't without talking about the funeral.

There are three rush periods at Bev's. Right before the last train people can catch to make it into Sydney before nine, at lunch and after school. It's a shitstorm the first day, but I get the hang of it. I realize if I burn their milk one morning, they'll only order a bagel the next.

Bad for Bev, good for Harley.

I check my phone when it's quiet. Jacs still texts.

JACS
Turns out my sister's pregnant.
Worried she'll go full-on trash with the name.
I don't think I can love a Shane.

It reminds me of Sue. I lean against the coffee machine. I have her contact entry open. My finger hovers over Dial.

"Did you go to Kiama?" I didn't even notice the guy waiting to be served. "Scott Harley, right?"

I force a smile at him.

"I knew it was you." He squints a little. "I thought you went off to some fancy Sydney school. What are you doing here?"

JACS
What are you doing?

Working. I'm working. I'm…sneaking out the back to make a call.

Bev pops her head out the door. "We need you in here," she says.

"One sec," I mouth.

I'm sitting on a milk crate next to the bin with my

phone to my ear. Five calls to the *Herald Daily* and still no progress.

"I get that the article's weeks old, but it's the first thing that comes up when you search his name."

The receptionist tells me to leave my number.

"I already did that and no one got back to me…"

I give up on making calls. Jacs still texts.

JACS

The seventh-grade production of Animal Farm… Holy crap, I haven't laughed so hard in my life.

Tears. Literal tears.

I imagine Jacs cackling at the shitty play while I burn the milk on purpose. Someone passes the window. Someone I know. I put down the jug and vault over the counter. I trip a bit, recover mostly and stumble out of the bakery. The sky's bruised purple and pink, and his gray tracksuit practically screams.

"Thommo?" I call.

The guy looks back at me and I stop. He has a stubbled mustache.

Definitely not Thommo.

"Ah. Thought you were someone else… My bad."

JACS

I thought I saw you on George St. today.

It wasn't you, was it?

It wasn't. I haven't left Gerringong in weeks. I wake, I work, I sleep. Nothing exciting, but exciting's overrated.

I wake, and there's a letter from Barton on the breakfast bar, dated last Friday. I skim it...*in regards to Scott's protracted absence...missed assignments...how to best facilitate Scott's return...Kathleen Evans*. Her signature's a mess.

Dad comes in, carrying a basket of dirty laundry. "They want to know when you're going back," he says.

"I got that."

He clears his throat. "Any idea when that might be?"

JACS

I don't know if you're getting these.

I hope you are.

I miss you.

———

Jacs sits on the edge of the Archibald Fountain. She's on her phone. The plan's to say something casual to make her look up, but before I can, she looks up on her own. Her forehead knots like she doesn't believe I'm standing here.

"Hi?" I try.

She launches off the fountain's edge and rushes at me. She throws her arms around my neck. "I was convinced..." Her breath is short. "I was convinced I'd never hear from you again and... You're back."

She pulls out of the hug and punches one fist into my chest.

"Ow!"

There are more punches, one for each word. "You. Can't. Vanish. Like. That."

I pull back. "Jesus, Jacs."

She blows a stray hair out of her face and sits back on the fountain's edge. I sit next to her but not as close as I used to.

"Look, I get it," she says. "Zac died. It's shit. But what you did, you control that. You didn't say goodbye. You didn't... Not even one text. You dropped me."

"I dropped everyone."

She shakes her head. "I deserve more from you than that."

"I'm sorry."

"Damn right, you are."

A thought hits me. "Wait, have you been sitting here every morning, waiting for me?"

She rolls her eyes. "Yeah, I'm a regular Miss Havisham."

"Who?"

"Dickens character, dumped at the altar, sits in her wedding dress for the rest of her life. Based on an Australian chick."

"Seriously?"

"Yup. Visited her grave near Newtown. The more you know." She leans in a bit. "No, I haven't been sitting here. I just knew the text was good."

"That's...manipulative."

"And ignoring me isn't?"

She won't let me forget anytime soon. Not to burst her bubble, but it wasn't just the text. There was other stuff...

"Dad was threatening to have Mom come sort out my life," I tell her. "And I was definitely about to get fired. I'm not a very good waiter."

"Never thought you would be."

I laugh. She smiles.

Without looking down, she adds, "Your fly's undone."

———

When I see the familiar white four-wheel drive, I push off the tree. The car rolls to a stop, the passenger window comes down and Sue leans over. She looks past me, into the café she recommended for lunch.

"It's a bit of a shitshow in there, isn't it?" she asks.

I blink. When Jacs left for school and I called Sue to suggest lunch sometime, I didn't think she'd want to do *today*.

Sue glances at her rearview mirror. There's a car in her lane that isn't slowing down. She clears junk off the passenger seat with a swipe of her arm. "Get in," she says.

I open the door and I'm careful not to step on anything.

"Don't worry about that crap. I keep telling Warwick this isn't his office." Sue releases the hand brake and accelerates before I've got my seat belt on. "It's a shame—that place does really nice salads," she explains, eyes on the road. "I'm sure your mother would have appreciated me taking you there. But now that I think about it—

me getting a parking spot, and then us finding a table—going there was a flight of fancy."

"I assumed you'd just walk from work."

"No, I'm twenty minutes from here. I told them to go to hell and that I'd be taking the afternoon off."

I laugh. "Seriously?"

"No, I…" She takes a breath, then begins again. "I told them I was seeing my son's friend, and they've been very accommodating."

That's the reality check. And all I've got to meet it is "Oh." Sue's better at pushing past it. I reckon she's had more practice. She changes the subject. "So, why aren't you at school?"

"I went home for a bit, spent some time with Dad."

The cogs of Sue's brain churn. "You're down south, aren't you?"

"Yeah."

The cogs churn some more. "You didn't come in just for lunch, did you?"

I owe her.

"No, I was on my way back."

"Good, because otherwise I'd feel guilty about doing this." Sue takes the next left and parks outside the massive gas station with the built-in burger place.

I save a booth by the window. Sue returns from the counter with two meals, and when she sits, she empties our fries into one heap on the tray. "I'm only going to have a few," she says.

I grab my carton and pop it open. She's ordered me

a double cheeseburger, but it's a bit of a stretch to say something so small is double anything.

"They shrink every year," Sue says, lifting hers. The cheese has melted up one side of the bun. "What a sad little thing." She takes a bite and then quickly takes another. "Tasty, though."

I bite into mine. She isn't lying.

She smirks as she chews. "Do you—?" She reconsiders, swallows and starts again. "Do you remember the first night we met?"

I draw a blank. From this far, all the times I crashed at Zac's have blurred into one.

"You and Isaac went out after we went to sleep."

"Oh." I remember it in parts... Marty's parents were away for the weekend, he had a party, Zac and I hit the bottle hard, snuck back in around two...

"I have never heard two people make so much noise in my life," Sue says.

"We were stealthy."

"You managed to wake the neighbor's dog."

"That's right! We were raiding the pantry. He wanted popcorn."

Sue nods. "I was finding kernels on the floor for a week."

"And when you came down..." I remember thinking she'd blow up. Mom would of, but Sue didn't. She sat Zac down at the dining table and sent me to bed with a glass of water. When I woke up, Zac was still downstairs. I could tell they hadn't moved all night. They were playing cards. When Sue noticed me, she pushed up off the table and asked what we wanted for breakfast. "What was with that?" I ask. "I mean, I know it's a punishment, but I don't think I get it."

Sue sighs and puts down her burger.

"When you're pregnant," she says, "everybody tells you it will all click as soon as the kid pops out. Baloney. You have an inkling. You remember what your parents did wrong, and you try not to do that. You read the books, so you know what the experts say, but when you're in that room with this fragile thing, you're on your own. You don't really know what you're doing, but he relies on you, so you just do it. And you give him everything you have. You love him like he's still this fragile baby, even when he has BO and talks back to you. But as much as you want to, you can't be there all the time, and, well..." It's like she's stolen all the air out of the world and it's hard to breathe. She gasps and blinks down at her lap. "He was drunk—you both were. He was in the ninth grade, but he'd grown up. I knew whatever line there was before adulthood, he'd crossed it. In the morning, he'd be different, we'd be different. I didn't want to yell at him, I didn't want to send him up to bed, I didn't want to waste my chance to stretch his childhood just that little bit longer. So, we played Go Fish, like we used to."

Sue clenches both fists for a second, like she rips herself from there and then, the dining table opposite Zac two years ago, to here and now, the booth of a fast-food restaurant attached to a gas station.

"I wasn't punishing him." Her voice cracks. "He was

on the edge of the rest of his life and I wanted to sit there with him. It was…" She can't find the right word, so she leaves it as is. "It was."

She blinks away and raps her knuckles on the table. "Isaac would probably tell me I'm embarrassing him," she says.

"No…"

She smiles a little, which makes my chest feel less heavy. "Don't lie."

"I'm not."

"It's what mothers do." She grabs a fry. "I'm sure yours embarrasses you regularly."

"*Mm.*" I can't tell her we're not close. That'd be insensitive. She's broken up over losing what Mom and I have tossed away.

It's not the same, though.

Sue waited up with Zac.

Mom left. She didn't even offer to take me with her.

On a street of town houses, the boardinghouse is a string of six merged into one—dorms upstairs, communal areas downstairs. It never used to be yellow; that's new. There's always something to paint or renovate at Barton.

I press my student ID against the sensor by the door. The lock whirs and I let myself in. It's half past two. No one's around. Guys won't start trickling in for another hour, and Olive and Jo won't be in till four. I raid their fridge. Two bananas and a tub of yogurt with Toby written on the side.

My dorm's the closest to the stairs. I work the handle with my elbow and lean into the door till it opens enough to slip through. Without me keeping him in check, Hughes has taken over the entire room. My bed's covered in his crap—soccer gear, crumpled shirts, underwear. I scoop it all in a heap.

When he wanders in at five, he asks who dumped his shit on the floor. Then he sees me lying on my bed, one leg crossed over the other, polishing off Toby's yogurt.

"Ah. Sorry, man," he says. "We thought you weren't coming back."

———

We have dinner at senior citizen o'clock. It isn't even dark outside. The other juniors ask questions, but I brush them off. Collins makes this big scene, raises his glass, welcomes me back. Corny as hell.

———

I'm up and showered by six thirty to avoid Collins's countdown. The dining hall is dark. It's just me and the sound of Olive and Jo trading barbs and cackling in the kitchen. There's nothing in the buffet yet, so I grab a banana from a bowl on the nearest table and duck out.

It's drizzling, not enough to warrant heading back upstairs to fetch my umbrella, but enough that if I see someone with their own, I'm gonna sneak under. I buy a coffee from a hole in the wall on the way and nurse it. When I get to Barton, Evans is bantering with the ladies at the front desk. I step through the sliding doors and her eyes zero in on the large cup in my hand. I stand frozen. Her eyes follow the cup as I slowly slide it inside my blazer. I hold it there and watch her. She watches the coffee-shaped lump beneath my uniform.

"I'll drink it quickly, miss."

"You had better." I go to weave around her when she holds out her arm to stop me. "Before you… I've asked Mr. Ford to make some time to see you this morning."

"Now?"

"Ideally."

I kind of wish she'd confiscated my coffee and been done with it.

I must look pissed. She smiles. "Welcome home, Scott."

———

The Twelvies have one volume: loud. Seventh-grade kids can't get wet or they melt or some shit, so they're all crammed in the hallway, screaming at each other. I charge through them. I remember coming down this way with Evans, my first week at Barton. She was taking a group of us to an after-school detention cleaning a Visual Arts room. Zac walked beside me, pale and freckled like the moon with the measles.

"Haven't you only been here, like, two days?" His mouth hung open; his braces alternated between purple and silver from tooth to tooth. "What'd they get you for?"

"Skipped sixth period on Wednesday. Went to the movies."

"Alone?"

"What did you do?"

"I walked into Mr. Sheldrick's German class and asked what year it was. When a kid told me, I was all like, "My time machine worked!""

"That got you a detention?"

He hesitated. "I try to interrupt at least one of his classes every day. We have a special relationship. He hates me, and I try to give him a nervous breakdown."

"That's…weird."

He shrugged. "I'm Isaac."

I misheard. "Zac?"

"Isaac," he repeated.

I shrugged. "Zac's better."

I collide with a pack of Twelvies hanging by the door to the yard. It's still raining. They can't decide whether to grow a pair or stay inside. I look out. There's a row of dickheads passing a rugby ball and some loner sitting on a bench in the corner.

Thommo.

Thommo came with Zac. What we have is mostly built on him being more tolerable than Miles. I mean, sure, there's that sweet spot between three and four drinks where we click, one-on-one, but that's it.

He's a swimmer.

It's his out for everything. The break we met, Olive

and Jo packed me way too much chocolate cake, so I offered him some. "I'm a swimmer."

My reply was instant. "Oh. Lucky. This kid back home ate mud cake, drowned the next day." And that's become our blueprint. When he takes himself too seriously, I just knock him down a peg. He's a swimmer. I'm a joker.

We're not close, but I thought I saw him in Gerringong and fell over myself trying to get to him. Which is weird. I dunno, it's kinda like there's this pull…

I sweep the Twelvies aside with an arm powered by puberty and push open the door. It's chilly, but that's what the coffee's for. I sip and walk.

Thommo's scratching at the table. He looks beat. I go to ask what's wrong but lose my nerve.

"Jeez, who died?" I ask instead. I sip my coffee. "I'm back."

"I can see." He straightens up and pops his chest out. Look at those pecs. I bet he's a swimmer. "You been good?"

It's not the sort of question you answer truthfully. "Yeah, had fun back home."

"Sweet." He does a neck roll. His muscles must be tight. Just a hunch, I think he's a swimmer. "I'm okay."

"Good."

"Yeah."

And there's a sec where we stare at each other.

"Well, I've got to go." I point over my shoulder, back the way I came. "Evans wants me to see Ford. I just came over to…" I trail off. I came over; I didn't walk past. I came over on purpose.

And I don't know why.

"Just on my way, that way." I point past him, at nothing.

"Right."

Ford wants to have a casual chat. He isn't wearing a tie. I know. He has lots of questions, none of them about Zac. He wants to know how *I've* been, what Dad's been up to, whether I've heard from Mom. He starts talking about the cultural ethos of Barton, the support network. Then someone knocks at the door. A kid in eighth grade who was supposed to see him at lunch but can't cuz of Band, and...

I tune out. My eyes wander right, to a shelf cluttered with stuff from a recent Nepal trip, framed family portraits and a collection of Barton House function programs— all marble-stained A4 sheets folded once and formatted the same. Their covers have the school crest and then, in the same tired font, the school motto, the event name. Sports Assembly. Father and Son Breakfast. Isaac Roberts in Memoriam. The program from Zac's funeral. I never saw it on the day.

I open it up. The order of ceremony is interrupted by photos of Zac, from toddler to teen. I turn to the back and there's a photo of us, hanging outside the movies, our drinks cropped out.

The door shuts. Ford starts apologizing and I slip the program between my seat and my bag.

I have double Business Studies first. It all happens as per usual. No one takes their books out cuz no one gives a shit. I sketch a potential tat in the margins of my planner while Buchannan takes the roll. He works his way from Anderson. When he gets to me, he welcomes me back with a nod. After Okins, he moves right through to Smith.

"He's on his way," Okins answers.

He skipped past Roberts. That's how it is now, I guess.

I leave the tat unfinished.

Buchannan lets us out a couple of minutes into break. Guys are trying to do whatever they usually do outside inside, to avoid the rain. The hall's a mosh pit that reeks of body odor laced with cologne.

I use the subtle art of persuasion to get a guy off my locker. "Move."

I enter my combo, and force of habit, I look over at Zac. We'd be shouting the end of our Business Studies conversation, but he isn't there. His locker's open. A kid tosses in his chocolate wrapper.

"Hey!"

He doesn't hear. I bulldoze the world between us. I pull him around by the shoulder. I recognize his face. He's in the grade below, Devon or Daniel or—

"Dickhead, what was that?"

His face is all screwed up. "What was what?"

I open 308. There's a half-eaten sausage roll on a bed of wrappers in there. They're using it as a makeshift trash can.

"Do you even—?" It gets caught in my throat. Dickhead and his friends blink at me. The stupid xylophone bullshit bell starts, and the guys take off.

One of them coughs, "Loser."

While the others open their lockers, I find the nearest trash can and pull out the liner. It's heavy and its contents swish. I claw the crap out of 308 and into the bag.

Noah unlocks 310.

"Have you seen this?" I ask him.

"Yeah."

Does everyone seriously not give a shit? Is that how quickly this place forgets someone?

I drop the heavier bag back in the bin and go to my locker. I grab the crumpled program I swiped from Ford's office and turn to the back. I tear from the bottom, around the pic of Zac and me.

I lean out. There's a line of bodies half-in lockers. "Does anyone have tape?" I ask.

There's no response.

"Tape?"

A hand swings back with a roll in it. I pull off two strips.

"Thanks." I'm already walking.

I slap the photo against 308 and tape the sides down. Let them try to forget him now.

———

Collins stands up at dinner. I bury my face in my hands, anticipating another toast.

"Gents, as you are no doubt aware, tomorrow we will be entertaining the lovely ladies from Sacred. The seating arrangements are up on the wall. Familiarize yourself with your spot before then. And it goes without saying, we expect quality behavior from each and every one of you."

Yeah, good one.

The boarders snigger. For most of them, it's their only exposure to the opposite sex beyond teachers and the catering ladies. When confronted with Sacred chicks, they either act like total dicks or collapse into themselves and wait for the girls to go away. It's like watching baby animals trying to walk for the first time, but the teachers keep organizing it, probably for a laugh.

———

I take the scenic route to second-period Visual Arts. I pass Zac's locker on the way and stop. There's a second photo, stuck to the left of mine. Two guys by the pool, one in a Speedo, the other dressed and wholly unimpressed by the wet arm around his shoulder.

Thommo put up his own pic. I look from Zac and me to Zac and Thommo… The pictures rhyme.

ME
You busy at lunch?

THOMMO

Yeah, I've got this thing.

ME

After school?

Or wait... You got Squad?

THOMMO

Nah, I'm free.

ME

You wanna hang out?

I should of been clearer, told him not to bring anyone else. I walk into the café and see Miles is with him. I wanna bail, but Thommo waves at me. As if hanging out wasn't going to be awkward enough, he's gone and invited a torture expert with a briefcase of pliers and shit.

Great.

"Yo." I dump my bag and fall into the chair.

Thommo says, "Hey."

Miles doesn't say anything. He looks.

I don't make memories of Miles. There's nothing worth keeping.

But I know he makes memories of me. Everything I do is filed away in that big mind he keeps telling us he has.

When he looks, I see what he thinks of me. I'm dumb. I'm a deadbeat. I'm some fucking tool. Just cuz I'm not in his box.

Just cuz I don't say "should *have*."

Yeah, he looks. But I live. And he resents that.

"So, how was your day?" I ask Thommo.

"Pretty uneventful."

He raises his glass and Miles looks.

"All right, if you're just gonna stare at me, out with it," I tell him. "Give me your worst."

"You killed him."

Thommo chokes on his water. "Shit," he coughs.

Miles's eyes are vacant. I push down the guilt. I suppress the thought of Sue without a son. I am not wounded. My eyes are blank.

"That's it?" I ask. "What else you got?"

I wonder how many times he's rehearsed what he'd say if he ever saw me again.

"You only thought about what was good for you. Whatever he asked for, you got for him. He overdid it and you never had the guts to pull him up, because he was your ticket to a place you could crash on the weekends."

Thommo inhales, wide-eyed. The waiter approaches. I tell him we're not ready. He wanders off and I lean in. "Is that really what you think?"

"Yes." Miles sits tall. "You pushed us out."

Thommo shakes his head. "Don't drag me into this."

I work with it. "He was there."

"Me, then," Miles corrects himself. "You pushed *me* out."

"*Mm.*" I cock my head to one side. "You're a wet blanket, Miles. And all you can do with a wet blanket is leave it out to dry."

It hits harder than I expect. His voice trembles. "That is not fair."

"Not as fair as saying I killed him?"

"You were his dealer," Miles snaps.

My eyes narrow. "And you were the alternative."

Miles stammers. I ease back. Thommo says, "Christ." He pulls the laminated menu out from under my elbow and turns it over. Seeing this, the waiter kicks off the wall. "This ends now. We're breaking bread." The waiter gets to us before Thommo's had time to peruse. "Do you have bread?"

"We have croissants?"

Thommo blinks. "We're breaking croissant."

"One croissant?" the waiter asks.

"With three plates."

"They're very small." He mimes the croissant's size.

"Then bring small plates," Thommo says.

"Anything to drink?"

"I'm okay with water."

"Espresso," I say.

"Orange juice, please," Miles croaks.

The waiter takes the menu. We don't say anything. He returns with the croissant on one side plate and two spares. Thommo breaks the pastry and gives us each a third. He reconsiders, breaks his in half and then halves one of those pieces. He gives one to Miles and one to me. Cuz he's a swimmer.

"Do you remember House Competition Day?" he asks.

Miles furrows his brow, and then an "Oh" and a nod.

The teachers are always lax with attendance on House

Comp Day. We had dodgeball the period before lunch.
Zac convinced us to throw our games, get eliminated and
explore the city for a few hours. Miles too. We ended up
at a liquor store attached to a bar. Thommo, Zac and I
went in. Zac grabbed a six-pack and walked straight to
the counter in his uniform.

"Look, man, I know this looks suspicious," he said,
speaking through his bottom teeth to sound older.

The owner didn't let him say more. "Out, or I call
the cops."

Zac gave him a curtsy. "Good day to you, sir."

And we bailed.

Thommo shakes his head. "Can't believe he thought
that'd work. Such a moron."

"I can't believe Miles played hooky."

Miles is quick to his own defense. "Well, I was not
going to drink anyway."

Thommo rolls his eyes. "Oh, get off your high horse
for a minute. You and Zac were selling black-market
essays."

I pick up my croissant. "What?"

"Oh, yeah. They had an underground operation going.
Made thousands."

"Hundreds," Miles corrects.

"Fuck me." I'm impressed. "I thought Zac told me
everything."

"He definitely didn't," Thommo says. "Thanks."

The waiter's put our drinks down in the center of the
table. I pick up my coffee and Miles slides his juice closer.
He leans in. He misses the straw and chases it around the

glass with an open mouth. He gets it eventually. And sucks on it, accomplished.

"But yeah, the takeaway from today is," Thommo says, "Miles would pay Isaac to be the face of his illegal essay empire, and Isaac would then pay you for narcotics. So really, if anyone's blameless in all this, it's me."

"That is not funny," says Miles.

But he's the first to laugh.

——————

The gate sings on its hinges as it shuts. "Are you sure it is okay for us to be here?" Miles asks.

I press my card against the sensor. The lock whirs. "The straight-A student, the son of a teacher and me. I'm pretty sure if they have to choose between us, they'll kick me out." I push the door open.

"What's the worst they're gonna do?" Thommo asks. "Send us home? *Ooh!*"

"Just stick with me," I urge. "You'll meet some chicks. Try not to act like yourself."

"I have a girlfriend," Miles says.

"Sure you do."

The dining hall is divided by gender. In the rec corner, the Sacred chicks swarm around the billiards table, while a handful of them try to play pool in the gaps. The guys are either in their assigned seats or part of the huddle around the cardboard seating chart. It doesn't take that long to find your spot—they're just freaking out about the girls they're sitting with.

I pull out the closest seat. Thommo does the same. Miles hesitates.

"It is assigned seating, though?"

"No one ends up sticking to it," I tell him.

"Surely they will realize…"

On cue, Collins turns away from the catering ladies and notices I've brought company. Miles shits a brick. I wave. Thommo tries not to laugh. Collins excuses himself and comes over.

"Suppress all of your instincts," I mutter to Miles. When Collins is close enough, I say, "Hey!"

"Gents, I didn't know you boarded with us."

Miles starts, "Sir, I—"

"They're your responsibility, Harley. They misbehave, you're on kitchen duty for a month." His eyes narrow for a sec. "Your parents know where you are, right?"

They both nod.

"Then don't embarrass yourselves." He smirks and moves over to the huddle by the seating chart. "Disperse! Be sociable!"

Miles exhales.

"Dude, you're weak as hell," I say.

"Shut up."

Jacs swoops into the opposite seat. "Took your time," she says. She probably recognizes Thommo from photos. I don't think their paths have ever crossed at gatherings, though. She turns to Miles, intrigued. "You're new."

"I am Miles."

"He has a girlfriend," I add, pulling the appropriate face.

"Hello, Miles who has a girlfriend, I'm Jacqueline."

"That is my aunt's name. But she is dead now."

I go for stunned silence. Thommo cackles. "Dude, you have negative people skills. Like, less than none."

Jacs leaps to his defense. "Says the guy who's clearly here because he can't meet girls otherwise."

Thommo keeps it chill. "I'm just here for the food."

She nods slowly. "Gotcha." She isn't a subtle operator and I can see her lining up a shot. "Don't worry, I'm happy to lie about how we met."

Thommo lobs it back. "I wouldn't admit to meeting anyone here either."

She shifts in her seat. It's game on. "What's our origin story, then?"

I don't reckon Thommo can conjure some fake history from thin air. Just as I go to say something about how weird it is to be back, he conjures it.

"You tried to take the last watermelon at the supermarket but gave it to me because I was heading for it. Nothing else, not till we bumped into each other again at the checkout and you asked me out for coffee," he says.

She clicks her tongue against the roof of her mouth. "You're smart."

"Thanks."

"Your story doesn't hold up, though. Nobody who knows me would believe I'd willingly give away the last watermelon. I'd have a Quarter Quell over that shit." She makes herself laugh with that one. I smile, but she doesn't look away from Thommo. It feels...off. "And where do you live?"

"East."

"I board down the street. Why would I be at your supermarket, buying a watermelon? I get all my food from school, and if I didn't, why would I trek to your local only to have to carry a watermelon back here?" she asks. "It falls apart under basic scrutiny."

I swoop back into the conversation. "Jacs wants to be a lawyer."

"*Will be* a lawyer," she corrects. She turns to me. "How's it feel to be back?"

———

Everyone's a bit slow coming down for breakfast. I have the table to myself, so I draw. Nothing special, just random shapes on my napkin, which I hide when Hughes shows up. Everyone dresses for school before breakfast. He's in his baggy hoodlum tracksuit and his eyes are barely open. We have the morning off every second Friday. It's scheduled as double Math, which is double a subject we don't take. This isn't one of those Fridays.

"Confuse your Fridays?" I ask.

"Yup." He pours milk into his cereal and starts eating. "Why'd your alarm go off so early anyway?"

"Cuz I didn't confuse my Fridays." Coffee with Jacs, actually. "Ah, crap."

Hughes's mouth hangs open and a little milk escapes. "What?"

"Incoming."

He checks over his shoulder. Toby Caroline with a bowl of cereal. He's in the year below, but he always tries to sit with us. We're "more his level." Someone told him he was mature for his age once. I want to slap that person.

"Hey," he says.

"Hello, Toby." I deadpan it, but it goes right over his head. It always does. He slips into the seat beside Hughes.

Usually, we're safe at breakfast. He's in Squad. But for some reason, the universe has decided to bless us with his presence. He's probably sick and about to share the germ love.

"How'd it go last night?" he asks.

Hughes fields the question. "All right."

"Did you...you know?" Pro tip: if you call it you-knowing, you're not mature for your age.

"Yeah, right on the table halfway through dinner—didn't you see?"

"Really?"

Hughes's eyes widen.

"Oh, you're kidding?" Toby asks.

"Yes," Hughes groans.

Toby finally senses the hostility. He turns to me. "How about you?"

"No sex for me, but my friend did hit it off with one of the girls."

"Who? Ryan?"

I nod.

This puzzles Toby. "But he's gay."

I snort a laugh. Seriously, this kid... "No, he's not."

"He is. He told me."

I nod. "Sure he did."

"No, seriously. Before swimming the other day. He thought I was and he told me."

"You know," Hughes chimes in, "I'd buy it."

"See?" Toby says. "What? You're saying he's never put the moves on you?"

"No. And trust me, he's not."

Toby's adamant. "I'm telling you, dude, he is. Not that there's anything wrong with it. I mean, my cousin is. It's cool."

Hughes twists his face a bit. "We had PE together years ago. I wonder if he ever stared at my junk in the locker room."

"Who?" Fuzz asks, a piece of dry toast hanging from his mouth. He sits on the other side of Hughes.

"No one," I tell Fuzz. "He didn't stare at your junk," I tell Hughes.

"Ryan's gay, apparently," Hughes explains.

"There's nothing wrong with it, though," Toby re-iterates.

Fuzz says he isn't surprised. He didn't pick it, but he isn't surprised.

———

Jacs waits at the fountain. She has two cups by her side. She hands me one as I sit. "Last night was fun," she says.

Looking back on it, it was. I nod a couple of times.

She's watching me closely. "Your friends are cool."

I'd tell her they're not my friends, if it wasn't such a Miles thing to do.

"Well, maybe *cool* is the wrong word," Jacs says. "*Interesting*. They're interesting."

"Miles has a girlfriend."

"Oh." Jacs covers her grin. "I feel bad for laughing. Poor guy."

"I don't. It's hilarious."

She lets herself laugh a bit and then looks down. "So… what's Ryan's deal?"

That's traveled fast, even by boardinghouse standards. I'm about to tell her Toby's lying when she asks, "Does he have a girlfriend?"

Ah. She's into him.

It rubs me wrong. Not that I want to kiss her or anything. It's just, when Zac hung out with us, she didn't forget I was there.

"I dunno." I dunno if Thommo has a girlfriend. I dunno if Toby's telling the truth. I dunno.

"You don't know?"

"We're not really that close."

"You were both good friends with a guy who died— how can you not be close?" And then her eyes widen. Something suddenly makes sense to her. "You've still got the tat, don't you?"

"Yeah?"

"Knew it." She sips her drink.

"Knew what?"

"You think you're this macho guy who doesn't have roots and who doesn't care, who can just drop everyone and not return texts for *weeks*. But you do care, you do."

"We honestly have never been that close, Jacs."

"Are you saying you don't look at them and feel a little…" She pops her chest forward and grunts.

I make a face that's a question mark.

"A tug," she elaborates. "You don't feel like you're being pulled?"

I saw Thommo on the bench. Any other day, I would of just kept walking. But something made me go out and speak to him, even though I had nothing to say…

Jacs pulls on the elastic band around her wrist. "My pop used to stand in our kitchen, wearing his checkered flannel shirt and pajama bottoms with definite hip-hop swagger. He was too cool. Growing up, he'd say we spend our lives wrapping rubber bands around people. Some bands are so tight that you can feel them pulling you together. Some are loose and stretch for miles, there's so much give you hardly notice them. But you're still connected, and sooner or later…" She releases the band and it snaps back into her wrist. "Ow." She breathes in through clenched teeth and rocks forward. "That hurt more than I thought it would."

"I bet. You okay?"

"Yeah, I just won't explain it visually next time."

"Probably for the best."

She rocks back upright and exhales. "When he died, I didn't feel bad. You know why?"

"You're dead inside?"

She looks daggers at me. "When I asked which band he felt pulling him the hardest, he pointed from his heart to the earth. Grams."

I picture an old man acting it out with world-worn fingers. The image scratches at the base of my spine.

"We all have rubber bands. They don't make you any less you," Jacs says. "I mean, I texted and you crossed the country—"

"It's literally less than 80 miles."

"You crossed the country to come back to me," she says regardless. "You care."

"Shut up."

———

At break, I get to the bench first. I trace my finger over the corner where Zac scratched his initials until Thommo arrives.

"Hey," he says. I look up and this morning distracts me. Toby's flicked a switch in my brain, and now I don't just see Thommo—I see a collection of hints and suggestions, a guy who may or may not be gay.

He pulls himself up onto the bench and his thigh brushes against mine. I jerk my knee in. It's sudden, but I don't think he notices. He unwraps his tuna sandwich, I put down my empty cup. It's all very exciting.

"You haven't brought Miles with you. What gives?"

"He does his own thing at break."

"Good. He's a piece of work."

"He's…" Thommo chews on it. "Isaac was right. Everyone has a Hate Miles phase. You meet him and everything he does irks you. But you see something one day, and it all makes sense. I think I get him."

"Well, I hate him."

"It's just a phase."

"It's been a pretty long phase."

"He's fine. Yesterday was fine." He reconsiders. "It was fun, actually. Jacs is pretty cool."

Well, that's our coffee ritual ruined. I can see it now, me sitting on the fountain's edge beside an octopus fighting itself—Jacs and Thommo attached at the head, arms and legs flapping everywhere. I struggle to get a word in. An arm slaps my cup into the water.

Unless Toby's right.

"You into her?" I ask.

He laughs. "Yeah. Who wouldn't be?"

Shit. I mean, good on him. Jacs is awesome. You can't do much better than Jacs.

Toby's a dick. I shouldn't of let him get in my head.

My legs splay out a bit and I sink back onto my elbows.

"I could toss her your number, if you want?" I offer it like a no-obligation free trial of Scott Harley's friendship.

"Nah, you don't have to."

I fish my phone out of my pocket. "Seriously, it's no drama."

"It's fine."

"It'll take one second."

He laughs. He sounds more nervous than last time. "Dude!"

"What?"

I watch him. He's still smiling, but I don't believe it. Like he's straining. "No, I..." His eyebrows rise in the middle and his eyes go soft. He swallows hard and his face resets. "I just think she seems more like friend material, though."

And I feel bad for pushing. "Yeah, you're right. I completely get it."

––––––––

Three thirty hits and Buchannan's authority evaporates. It's the weekend. We fake the sound of sirens and there's a mad rush for the door. I loosen my tie as soon as I'm on the street. When I get to my dorm, my shirt and shoes are off. I fall onto my bed and trap myself in a loop of skateboard videos on my phone.

Jones pops his head in. "Collins says you've got a visitor."

This guy does an eighteen-foot ollie between two water towers. It plays back in slo-mo.

"Harley."

I look up. "Who, me?"

Jones curls his top lip. "Who else?"

Hughes isn't on his bed.

"But I don't know anyone."

"Well, there's some lady downstairs and she says she knows you," Jones says. He stomps off to his room.

Some lady? Honestly, I'm drawing blanks.

I leave my phone and hide the yogurt labeled Toby underneath my bed. I pop on a shirt and head down. Sue's standing in the doorway to the study.

Seeing her makes my chest hurt. Whatever elastic band I looped around her the first time we met, it had so much slack I never would of known it was there. She was Zac's mom. She let me crash some weekends. We waited for her to leave the room before we said anything important. Now I feel the elastic band.

"I know, I should have called," Sue says, "but I was nearby."

"No, it's cool," I say. "Hi."

"Hi." She checks around. "Can we talk?" She sounds severe.

Shit. She knows something. Why else would she come?

"Sure." I check the study. It's free. She follows me in and sits on the lounge. I lean against the opposite wall.

"I hope I'm not interrupting anything," Sue says.

"Well, it is chicken tandoori night."

"Oh, I can—"

"Kidding. It was a joke."

She laughs a little. "Well, in the interest of not wasting your time, I'll cut to the chase."

I want to delay it. "You don't have to."

She looks at me like it's a strange thing to say. "I can waffle on about something if you prefer?"

It's like I'm talking to Zac. I say so.

"Well, he didn't get his humor from his father, I can assure you," Sue says. "Anyway, I actually came by to ask a favor."

She's going to ask if I sold Zac drugs.

"Do you think you could, and feel free to tell me to take a hike, but do you think you could maybe, possibly, get the boys who were with Isaac that night to speak with me?"

I exhale so hard I deflate.

"I tried to reach out to them through the school, but Barton doesn't want to get involved, and the parents are being…" She scrunches her face. "If the roles were reversed, I'd… But that's all hypothetical. I have questions. Real questions. I've been thinking about it a lot since you and I had lunch. I don't like not knowing much about that night." She chews on a thought. "You don't know anything, do you?"

"No," I blurt.

"*Mm.*" She taps her knuckles on her thigh. "I just want to know what my baby's last hours were like."

———

My phone's screen lights up my corner of the dorm. It's pushing midnight and I'm in bed, scrolling through my conversations. I'm looking for the group chat with Marty, Ex and Omar. It's buried under weeks of new messages, just above my convo with Mom. I message them.

ME

What you guys up to tomorrow?

Dunno how I'll convince them to see Sue, but I'll worry about that when they're standing in front of me.

I quit the convo and tap Mom's. The last message was the morning I woke in Gerringong.

MOM

Your father called.

Hughes stirs. "Dude, it's like…" He gives up on figuring out how late it is. "Go to sleep."

I turn the screen brightness down. I'm staring at my convo with Mom. There isn't much to it before Zac died, a couple of questions from her and single-word responses from me. I'd never wanted to send more, but Sue… Every time I see her, I remember what I've done, why Zac isn't here anymore. If Mom didn't want to leave, she wouldn't of sent me here, I wouldn't of met Zac, I wouldn't of… None of this would of happened.

I want to ask what changed. We used to be tight. She used to say the most random shit. I used to love hearing her voice. She never lost her accent. She didn't sound like anybody else. If I still had that, I would still be in Gerringong and Sue would still have Zac.

I want to blame her. I want to tell her this is all her fault.

It's not. I'm the guy who knows a guy. It's on me.

But I want to hurt her for leaving. Same time, I want it to be like it used to. I want more than a couple of questions and single-word responses.

Jacs would say some shit about elastic bands. It's true. I feel ours tightening, pulling me toward Mom. Only I don't know what to say or how to start.

"Hey, Hughes?"

Silence.

"You awake?"

He makes an unfriendly sound. That's enough for me.

I can divvy up the boarders into two groups: ones whose parents live too far and ones whose parents are too rich. Hughes's folks are in London.

"Dude, what do you message your mom?" I ask.

"What are you talking about?" His words are muffled by the pillow.

"Like, what do you say to someone you don't see or talk to?"

"I just fucking message her."

Not sure what else I was expecting.

———————

Marty, Ex and Omar are spending their Saturday afternoon at Kev Tran's seventeenth barbecue. I hang by the bathrooms on the edge of the park. I pull my hood down and send a group text. Don't want anyone else to know I'm here.

The three of them look up from their phones at the same time. They walk over in a line.

"Dude, you should come over. The food is great," Ex says.

"I'm not here."

He laughs. "Look at you, all phantom and shit."

Marty tilts his chin in. "Do you have—?"

"No." I find I feel less like punching him in the face when I don't look at him directly. "I need you guys to man up."

Ex laughs. "What do you mean?"

"Zac's mom. She wants to know what happened that night."

"Um." Omar shakes his head. "Dad's lawyer said not to say anything."

I'm running out of faces I don't want to punch. "You're

not gonna get in shit. She just wants help filling in the blanks. For closure."

It's Marty's turn to laugh. "You want us to man up? We had to talk to reporters. We had to go see the coroner's counselor. Where were you? Not here." Asked and answered. His eyes narrow. "And what are we supposed to say? That our friend Harley ordered some low-quality shit and Isaac took it without telling us? Is that what she wants to hear?"

"That's not what I—"

"So you want us to smooth over that part?" Marty asks. "Stick our necks out but cover your ass?"

"No, I..."

"You what?" Ex asks.

"Yeah," Omar chimes in.

"I want you to tell her he was happy," I spit. "*That's* what I want you to do, make her think her son wasn't with three total fuckwits when he died."

———

Jacs breaks a corner off my brownie. "Don't look at me like that." She drops it into her mouth. "You should've eaten it faster."

Every couple of Sundays, she studies at the State Library. When she gives up after a few hours, she texts:

JACS
What's up?

We end up meeting in the library café. We order a brownie each, cuz we know there are proper meals waiting for us at our boardinghouses. She finishes first and steals some of mine. It's all pretty routine.

She hasn't mentioned Thommo yet. I'm glad. Don't know how to tackle it.

"Hey, isn't that your friend from the other night?" Jacs asks.

Ah, crap.

"The weird one," she adds.

I check over my shoulder. Miles is sitting three tables away. He's on his phone.

"That's him." I turn back and my brownie's gone.

Jacs tries to smile and chew at the same time. "Go over," she mouths.

"I'm good."

She stretches the elastic band around her wrist.

I don't budge. "Nope."

She releases the band and kicks me under the table. "Ow! Jeez. All right."

I budge. I walk over and say, "Hi."

He doesn't look away from his phone when he says, "Hello, Harley."

I glance at Jacs. She mimes me sitting down. I don't want to. She scowls. I sit.

"Had a good day?" I ask.

"Mm." He scrolls down.

"What are you reading?" I ask.

"An article." I fully expect him to just keep giving me the bare minimum, and then, out of nowhere, comes a full sentence. "I am not sure if you saw this when you went off the grid. They wrote an article about Isaac after he died. It comes up when you search his name. Half of it reads like an ad for the school, and in the other half, they interview your cronies."

Marty, Ex and Omar. They're not my cronies—they're more…essential others. Two guys drinking in a backyard is just sad, but five? That's a gathering.

"I come back to it, hoping there is something I missed."

"What do you mean?" I ask.

He slides his finger up and down the screen. "They mention Ryan. They backflip to mention Isaac was friends with 'a celebrated swimming champion.' Your cronies start their sentences with *we*, and you are a part of that, so they speak for you. But me? Nothing. It is like I did not factor into his life at all. Mrs. Evans says he was in the 'pilot young-filmmakers program.' I was accepted into the program, not him. I wrote the submission. I jumped through their hoops. I was selected. He just acted in my film. I understand that the school wants to mention their program and spin that he was a promising actor lost before his time, but could they not have tried to tell the full truth? Is acknowledging that I played any part in his life from seventh grade to now really that hard?"

"Not really."

"The way they write about the night, they keep it vague. They say…" He clears his throat and I know which part he's about to quote. I say it with him.

"Jumped or fell."

He stares at me. For a second, we're in sync. I feel the elastic band. It pulls me, and I swear it pulls him too.

"So you have seen it?"

"Yeah." I swallow hard. "I tried calling them to take it down. Can't get past reception."

That gets a smile out of him. "Maybe we need to storm the bassteal."

I laugh. "Yeah."

He sips his hot chocolate and I take out my phone.

Search: storm the bassteal

The search engine returns results for **storm the Bastille**.

———

I have first period off on Monday. Instead of heading to campus, I storm the Bastille—a massive tower near Wynyard Station. RBS Media's on level six. I follow the suits into the foyer, to the elevators that travel to the lower floors.

I'm the first person into the elevator. Everyone fills in after me and mine's the first stop. The doors open and nobody moves. There's some awkward maneuvering, then I'm out. The lady at reception is sitting on a tall stool at a taller desk. Behind her, several wall-mounted screens transition between the home pages of RBS's websites.

I pop my bag off my shoulder and approach.

How do you storm a Bastille without an angry mob? Make them think you're meant to be there.

The receptionist is too bubbly for how early it is. "Hello there."

"I'm here to see the editor." I tap my knuckles on her desk.

She opens a messaging program, clicks the search field and asks, "Which one?"

I blink at her. "Which one?"

"Yes, which editor?" Her hands hover over her keyboard.

"Oh. The main one."

Her brow creases. "Is someone expecting you?"

I hesitate. "Not exactly."

"I see." She pulls her hands back. "Our editorial staff don't usually meet with readers in person. They're exceptionally busy."

"No worries, I can wait. I'm free till, like, half past nine. I'll just set myself up over here." I'm already dragging my bag to the quirky Mad Hatter's tea party setup tucked to the side.

"Sir, that's not... Sir?"

I sit in the massive armchair by the window and check my nails, cuz that's what people who don't give a fuck do.

"Hello, Frank."

I look up. She has her headset on. She explains the situation to some guy named Frank and then responds to whatever he says back with sounds.

"He has a backpack, but he's a schoolkid, so I don't think that's... Fifteen, I think." She makes a couple more active-listener sounds and then says, "All right."

I perk up. That seems promising.

The receptionist peels off her headset and comes around the desk. Her heels clack a path to me. She smiles. "I just spoke to my manager. Unfortunately, all the early-morning staff are tied up in the pitch meeting."

"I can wait."

"He'd like me to call security."

———

I wait by the main entrance. I'm not ready to cave and say I failed. I can't undo Mom sending me to Barton. I can't stop myself from finding the number scratched into my bed. It happened. Zac died. But they don't have to say he *jumped*. That sounds like he did it to himself.

I have the *Herald Daily*'s Meet the Team page open on my phone. There are serious black-and-white pics slammed against quirky bios. ("Calvin Briggs is our political editor. He likes heated arguments, hamburgers and Fridays.") It makes me hate Calvin and his friends, but I look for them. When I see anyone who sorta looks familiar, I scroll through the bio pics, and I'm either wrong, or they're already gone.

I have to give it my best shot. If I'm late to second period, so be it. I'll come up with a good excuse.

———

"Sorry I'm late, sir. Couldn't find my shoe."

Thommo's a no-show at break. I spend it lying on the bench, getting rays. Evans comes past, says it's a bench, not a sunbed.

I sit up. She's walking around the yard, flanked by a guy in a flannel shirt and jeans. She leads him through the cluster of benches and I eavesdrop. "The boys hardly use these at breaks anymore, as you can see. They eat in the halls, where they're closer to the power outlets and air-conditioning. I would love to transform this whole corner into an oasis. Some greenery, built-in stools. Something more alive. So even if they're not out here, at least it looks good."

"Let me see." The guy starts sketching with one finger on his tablet.

"You're getting rid of the benches?" I ask Evans.

She glances back at me. "Not *getting rid of*, repurposing."

Sounds like splitting hairs.

"The boys taking Industrial Tech will have a field day stripping them back and recycling the timber."

The guy tilts his tablet so she can see.

"Yes, something like that, only…" Evans explains her vision in more detail.

I stare at Zac's initials scratched into the corner of the table.

I pass Miles in the hall and ask if he's seen Thommo.

"Ryan was not in Modern History this morning." I

wonder if anyone's ever told him about *wasn't*. "He is probably sick."

Miles tries to run off to homeroom. Before he can, I ask, "How was the rest of your Sunday?"

"What are you doing?"

"My night was all right. A bit slow."

"Please stop."

"What?"

He sighs. "You and I are not friends, Harley."

"Not in the traditional sense, no, but we—"

"*We* did not get along when Isaac was alive. There is no reason to force it now." He tucks in his chin and walks off.

I feel the pull of the elastic band.

———

I dump my bag in the back corner of the room and sit next to Hughes. Mama Thommo watches from the front. Pill would of had to wait five minutes or do some clapping gimmick to shut us up, but with Mama Thommo, head of English, it's practically instant. It's her stare— makes me think all that kept her from becoming a contract killer was some quirk of fate.

"Right," she begins. "The more observant of you have noticed I'm not Miss Pill. Well done."

"Where is she?" Jai asks.

"That's none of your business. Has Miss Pill assigned you any work for this period?"

We all say, "No," in unison, except for Paul.

"What was that, Paul?" Mama Thommo asks, leaning closer to the guy sitting in the front row.

"Paul, you cock!"

The class laughs and Mama Thommo grimaces. "Charming."

"We're working through a past midterm exam paper this week, Ms. Thomson," Paul repeats.

"You don't say. Funny how the rest of the class forgot that." She walks to Pill's desk. "Papers out, get started. I have things to grade but I'll be poking my nose around later."

Hughes groans. "Trust us to get the one sub who'll actually make us do something."

Mama Thommo starts taking attendance and I check out. I stare at the patch of wall above the whiteboard. Between names, she tells me to start working. I groan and pull my bag closer.

"Try not to look like you've been wounded in battle, would you?"

I groan again.

"Shut up, Scott."

I have an exercise book I use for everything. It's covered in drawings, the corners have curled over, and there's a ton of loose sheets in the back. I flick through them, looking for the exam Pill gave us.

"Ms. T, what if I don't wanna work?" Hughes asks.

"Then you can make up the time at lunch," she says. "Would you prefer that?"

"But it's so gay."

I freeze and wait for her reaction. Does she know about Thommo? Is there anything to know?

She removes her glasses. "I don't understand. Do you mean it's a lighthearted, merry exam paper? Or is it attracted to exam papers of the same sex?" She pauses. "I'm hoping you don't mean it's pointless, boring and no fun, because for that, there are perfectly good words like *pointless*, *boring* and *no fun*. When you equate the way someone loves to something you don't like, you betray your limited vocabulary, which deeply offends me as head of English, and you harm your peers who may not love the way you do."

Someone says, "Shut down." I think it's the same guy who called Paul a cock. It doesn't get as many laughs.

"Relax, Ms. T. Most teachers let us say it," Hughes says.

"Well, they shouldn't," Mama Thommo snaps. "That's your sensitivity training done. Do your work."

"We don't care if anyone's gay. We're cool with Ryan. He can be whatever."

There's a sec where she doesn't say anything. Her eyes drift to me. Shit. This is the first she's hearing of it. My heart goes nuts and I try not to give anything away. She opens her folder.

"Mark, you're disrupting the class," she says.

Fuck. I need to get to Thommo. Now.

———

I tap the open door and Collins looks up. "Don't you have class?" he asks.

"Toilet break slash I wanted to double-check something. You're not allowed to give me another student's address, are you?"

"No."

"Okay." Never thought I'd ever regret not going to Thommo's seventeenth. A nonalcoholic movie night hosted by a teacher. Not my kind of party. It's exactly Miles's kind of party. Probably why *he* went.

"What room is Miles in right now?" I ask.

———

I loiter by the glass panel until Miles looks up from his work. His forehead creases. He thinks I'm trying to force a friendship, but whatever. This is bigger than that. I wave him over. He mimes, "No."

I insist. He shakes his head.

Fine.

I let myself in. Miles sits on the far side of the room, mortified.

Higgins asks if he can help me, and I ask Miles where Thommo lives.

Miles is flustered. "What? I—"

"Address. Write it on the bottom of that page and tear it off cuz I'm not gonna remember it."

He does as I say. I wave the piece of paper at Higgins on my way out.

———

Thommo lives on a street of giant fuck-off mansions with stone columns and seven-foot fences. His place is more of a modest fuck-off mansion. It's seriously lacking in the column department. But it's got the fence. Gold star for fencing. He'd be shit out of luck trying to sneak out of here on a Saturday night, that's for sure.

I watch the house through the bars of the gate as I press the intercom a second time. Thommo answers, "Yeah?"

"Open up."

"Who is it?"

I turn to the intercom and stare into the small black camera lens.

"Harley?" he asks. "Shouldn't you be at school?"

"Shouldn't you?"

There's a pause. And then the gate unlocks.

———

Thommo's taken the day off to work on an assignment. Doubt he's done much. He's been playing video games. He walks me into the lounge room and there's a mission paused on the TV. He sits on the lounge. I sit on the floor.

I ask about his weekend.

"You're being weird," he says.

"How?"

"This. You coming over randomly. It's weird."

I wanna say he's wrong, but he's not. The whole way here, I was certain I was doing what I had to. I was *pulled*. But now I feel like a phony, like I'm doing Zac's job, only worse. He would of been in Pill's class too—he would of come straight over, cuz he'd know Thommo's address.

There'd be no weirdness. It would of been as regular as me bumping into Jacs at the fountain.

But Zac isn't here, and I'm better than no one.

"You know, when I was younger," I say, trying to re-create Jacs's story as well as I can, "my granddad told me we wrap elastic bands around people. We're connected. Sometimes an elastic band is loose, then something happens and it, um…" I've lost it. Shit. "Look, Zac died. I reckon you and I are closer. Cuz he died for you too. Not *for* you—that makes him sound like Jesus."

"I get what you meant."

"Right." My throat's dry. "I wanted to say that, before—"

"I feel closer to you too," he says.

"Oh." I exhale. "You're gay, right?"

He coughs a laugh. "What?"

I'm direct with him. "You like dudes."

"No, I…" Thommo trails off. "How did you find out?"

I tell him about Toby, Hughes, his mom. That freaks him out. He springs to his feet and starts pacing. His breaths are short and shallow. He stops and doubles over, gasping for air. I can hear each breath scratch the back of his throat like sandpaper. I don't know how to comfort him, but I know I have to. I rest a hand on his back. It rises and falls with his body.

When I pull it off, he says it's helping, so I put it back.

I feel his lungs fill with air.

"Your mom was badass," I say. "She tore Hughes to shreds. He'll be shitting bricks for a week."

Doubled over, Thommo laughs into the next wheeze.

When he's calmed down, I go grab him some water. I almost get lost, but I find the kitchen eventually and retrace my steps. He drinks the water slowly and explains a lot of random stuff. It isn't a full history, but there's enough to understand. He sounds different when he speaks, like he's not acting anymore.

After all that, he tells me I can stay. "If you want," he adds. He points at the TV. "It's got multiplayer."

Tempting as it is, he needs to have a serious chat with Mama Thommo when she gets home. He walks me out, and two steps up the driveway, I turn back.

"Look, you're not alone," I say. He raises an eyebrow. I add, "You know where I live."

"Oh. For a sec, I thought you were gonna say something lame about Isaac being here to watch over me."

"As if I'd say that and as if he is."

"*Oooh*, I'm a ghost, I've returned to the land of the living to eavesdrop on intimate conversations about your sexuality, *oooh*!"

I laugh, right from the belly. Thommo smirks.

"He knew, didn't he?" I ask.

Thommo nods. "He did."

"He was a good guy, wasn't he?"

Thommo laughs. "No. But he did this stuff well."

"True." Something hits me. "This, today... Did I do all right?"

He nods. "Yeah, you did all right. Not amazing."

I flick him the middle finger. He lobs two back.

Hughes is lying on his bed when I walk in. "Houdini!" he says. "Where'd you go during English?"

"Nowhere." I plug my phone in to charge and look over at him. "Did you think she knew about Thommo?"

"No chance," he says.

I deserve a peace prize for not knocking his teeth out. He has Fuzz to thank for that.

"Hey, Harley." Fuzz is leaning into the room. "Collins wants you downstairs."

I find Collins in the study. He has my bag. I loop one arm through both straps and he asks where I was today in the deep voice he reserves for confiscating contraband. I tell him I was in the library. His face hardens. He knows I'm lying, but the truth means outing Thommo even more.

"I went to the movies, okay?"

I make a point of not sitting with the juniors at dinner. I set myself up in Siberia, the table furthest from the kitchen, and eat alone. Soon enough, though, I have my own harem of Twelvies, chewing with their mouths open and shrilly talking over each other in italics, like everything is *the most important thing ever.*

My phone vibrates. It's a wall of text from Sue:

SUE

When my old phone broke, I thought I lost everything. As it turns out, the sneaky bastards have been backing up my files in some cloud. Fancy that! A nice man in the store showed me how to download them. They brightened my day, I hope they do the same for you. Lots of love, Sue (Isaac's mom).

My phone vibrates again and a pic drops in underneath. It's Zac on Christmas morning, kneeling underneath the tree. He's wearing a paper crown and holding a champagne flute.

Not gonna lie, major feels.

Another pic drops in. In it, Zac poses cross-eyed behind his sister as she blows out her birthday candles.

A third one. Halloween, the year I met Zac. He's in a baseball uniform, Thommo's in a toga and I'm a zombie. We look funny as hell.

My phone vibrates.

SUE

Last one.

And there's the final pic. It's Zac and Miles, younger than I remember them. Their teeth are too big for their faces. They're taking a selfie in the back of class.

"You're not in seventh grade," the kid opposite me says. His teeth are also too big for his face.

I blink at him. "You're a prodigy."

———

Collins wants me to see Ford before school to chat about skipping yesterday, but I figure, if I'm already up shit creek with Barton, I might as well grab a paddle and start exploring.

ME
Coffee this morning?

JACS
Gimme 20.

ME
20 coffees?

JACS
Minutes. Jesus.

The cashier scribbles my order on two lids and leaves them for the barista. I wait near the coffee machine with the others. This one guy moves closer to the wall to make room for me and I swear I've seen him before. He's got these thick-rimmed glasses and… Holy flaming bag of shit from the sky.

I close my convo with Jacs and open the *Herald Daily*'s Meet the Team page. I scroll halfway down. It's him. Calvin Briggs, the political editor.

I play it chill. "Your name's Calvin, right?"

He jerks his head back and tries to place me. "Do I know you?"

"No, I…" I glance down at my phone. The screen goes dark. "I read your site."

"Oh!" That makes him smile. "Are you into politics?"

"Sure."

I'm really unprepared for this.

He's still smiling. "This is surreal. I've never been spotted before."

"Skim chai latte for Calvin?" the barista calls.

He grabs the drink and tells me how nice it was to meet a reader. He's leaving.

"Actually," I step into his way, "I've always wanted to know something. When you write a story and put it online, how long before you delete it…usually?"

"Oh, we never delete our content."

Damn. "Never?"

"Politicians and their handlers are always asking us to pull down stories," he continues, "but it's our policy not to. I mean, if we deleted everything we were asked to, there'd be no political stories."

"Oh."

He points his cup behind me. "Speaking of, those yarns won't write themselves."

I'm still blocking him. "I only ask cuz my best friend died in March."

"I'm sorry to hear that."

"There was a *Herald Daily* story about him. He fell and hit his head on a boat. You guys said he *jumped or fell*. Which made it sound like he meant to…" He meant to dive. He didn't mean to die. "If articles were deleted after a while, we wouldn't mind, but it's still there. I tried to get it changed, and there's this… Here, I'll show you." I bring up the article and tilt my phone so he can see. "If I go to the bottom…" He's watching when I click on the embedded video, Motorboat Bikini Babes.

"Is that…?"

"Girls dancing on a boat? Yeah."

Calvin squints at the screen. He has no idea why someone would put that… "Oh. It must be pulling it in because they've tagged the article with *motorboat*. The producer should've caught that before it went live," he says.

"Order for Harley?" the barista calls.

I ignore her. "Is there someone I can talk to about getting rid of it?" I ask.

"Oh, I can do that."

"Seriously?"

He nods. "Yeah, we use the same back end."

"Harley?" the barista asks.

"So you can get rid of the video and say he *fell*?" I confirm.

He hesitates. "Well, I can deactivate the video. As for changing the text, I'd have to speak to the news editors about it."

"There wouldn't be much to fix. I mean…" I scroll up through the article, searching for instances of *jumped or fell*. I catch a mention of the young-filmmakers program. The elastic band pulls.

Even if Calvin removes the video and changes *jumped or fell*, the article will still ignore Miles.

"How hard is it to add things?" I ask. "Cuz I've got this photo…"

———

Jacs and I sit on the fountain's edge, hunched over our phones.

She swipes her screen and gasps. "It's happened."

"What?" I refresh my browser.

———

"Aspiring actor with great potential—we are deeply saddened": Model student from one of Australia's most exclusive schools dies after "hijinks"

PUBLISHED MARCH 2 AT 1:55 PM,
UPDATED TODAY AT 9:13 AM

- Isaac Roberts fell from a motorboat early Monday morning, sustained head injury

- Drinking and "hijinks" with friends beforehand, police say

- Heartfelt tributes paid to much-loved sixteen-year-old

He *fell*. I sink back and breathe out. "He *fell*."
I scroll to the bottom. The video's gone, replaced by the pic of Zac and Miles. They're smiling. Their teeth are too big for their faces.

"The photo is pretty adorable," Jacs says.

It is.

"You're pretty adorable," she adds.

"What are you talking about?" I look up and our lips collide. Jacs is kissing me. I go with it. She puts her hand on my chest and breaks away.

"Huh?" It's all I've got. Where did that come from?

"Don't act surprised. It isn't hot."

"But you're into Thommo?"

"He's gay. Mark texted Cate."

Of course.

"So wait—I'm your backup?"

She tilts her head forward. "Seriously?"

I blink at her.

"Dude, I sat here every fucking day for weeks."

"You said you didn't."

"I lied!"

Oh. "Oh."

"You're aloof and you can be a bit of a tool, but I've tied a band around you, Scott. And I didn't realize how tight it was till you weren't here. I'd text you, and it was like I couldn't even—"

I lean over and kiss her this time. It's showy. I put my hand on one cheek. Hella romantic shit. I peel off her. Her eyes are still shut.

"I couldn't even breathe," she finishes.

———

I get to campus and it's almost break. I don't bother going to second period. I'm screwed no matter what. I might as well enjoy myself.

Thommo's sitting on the bench.

"What are you doing out here?" I ask.

"I've got a free," he says. "You?"

I hop up beside him and he assumes the worst.

"Mrs. Evans is gonna snap," he says.

"Let her. How'd last night go?"

"Perfect. Mom was…perfect."

They were up till one. He gives me the play-by-play. I smile, but it wrecks me knowing he gets something I don't. I take out my phone. After aimlessly cycling through my apps, I end up in my chat convo with Mom. I measure it against what he tells me Mama Thommo said. There's no contest. I mean, I haven't heard anything since Gerringong.

Do you think about me? I type.

My finger flexes to tap Send, but I hesitate. There's more to say.

Did I mess this up? Did you?

Thommo laughs and I nod along.

Was Australia ever real?

"When we were walking up to bed, Mom was like, "I've missed you." And I realized how long I've been hiding from everyone," Thommo says.

I blink at the questions. What good is all that mess, really? Whatever we haven't said… It's been so long, it's on us both.

I delete them and start over.

ME

I miss you.

I breathe out hard and lock the screen before Thommo sees.

"I guess I've gotta start telling people," he says.

"Probably."

"I wonder what Miles will say."

And I wonder if Miles has seen the article yet. Probably too soon, but I watch the doors across the yard for any sign of him.

THE NERD

EXT. ISAAC'S HOUSE—DAY

I stand on the driveway, in the dress shirt I have not worn since Christmas, and the skinny jeans that have fit me since, well, it is too embarrassing to say. A bag of groceries hangs from each hand. My grip is wet.

I take a breath.

I can leave, I know that. I can say I feel under the weather. I have done that before.

But I worry my next excuse might be one too many.

I walk. The front door is not completely shut. I push it open.

INT. ISAAC'S HOUSE—DAY

The corridor is dark. "Isaac?" I call.

The reply comes from upstairs. "I'll be a sec," he says.

I step in and lean back into the door until it closes. "Are you excited?"

The walls are closing in on me. I swallow hard. "Very."

"You should be." Isaac clears the final steps with a leap. He lands in a squat, sits deeper into it, and then launches up. He claps. "Today will be fantastic."

Isaac is wearing an orange safety vest and board shorts. I am overdressed.

"You will get burnt if we sit outside," I tell him.

"Ah!" He produces a stick of zinc from a pouch sewn into the vest.

"You will get burnt if we sit outside," I reiterate.

He streaks it across his face anyway. "Are you excited?"

"You already asked me that."

Isaac loops an arm around my neck. He knees a grocery bag. "Watch it," he says. He leads me deeper into the house. "I can't believe I've done it. I'm getting Miles Cooper shit-faced."

"Miles Cooper promised one drink."

"Shit-faced."

"One."

"Don't be such a wet blanket."

It cuts through me. I wear a smile, though.

He adds, "I don't get why you're so adverse to drinking." He means *averse*, but I do not correct him.

I begin to unload the shopping on the kitchen counter.

"What's all that, then?" he asks.

"Deli meats, a loaf of bread. I thought I would make us sandwiches."

"That won't be enough," Isaac says.

I run my eyes over the purchases. There is definitely enough for the two of us.

"Now, don't get mad…"

"Isaac."

Isaac grins. There are dimples. "I may have texted some of the guys."

"How many?"

He explains. With a handful of texts, our one-on-one has exploded into one of his famous gatherings.

I say, "Great." It is not nearly believable enough. I continue unpacking.

"You brought a book to a gathering?" Isaac asks.

One, there was never any mention of this being a gathering. Two, I do not trust anyone who leaves home without a book. It is just not right.

I change the subject. "I also brought organic kale chips so Ryan can eat something if he comes."

Isaac says it slowly. "Organic." He mouths it twice more, stretching the O.

I laugh. "You all right?"

Isaac's mouth hangs open, suspended in animation. He shakes it off and blinks at me. *"Hmm?"*

My chest hollows out. I tear my eyes away. "Nothing." I feign an interest in the kale chips' nutritional information. My forehead throbs. "Actually…" I look up at him. His eyes are vacant. "Are you high?"

"No." He loses a fight with a smirk. He laughs. "Okay, I might be a little."

"Isaac."

"What?"

"It is ten thirty."

"It's a gathering. What did you think we were going to do? Eat deli meats and read books?"

I smile. "You are right."

"Thank you."

The doorbell rings.

Isaac bounces on the spot. "Betcha that's Harley," he says.

"Are you going to get it?" I ask.

"I don't feel like he wants it enough," Isaac says.

I should laugh. All the pieces point to funny, but I can never get past him being...not himself. He chews on his bottom lip and cocks an eyebrow, and it just feels off. I look past him at the back door.

The doorbell rings a second time. "Hey! Zac!"

"You know, I think he's almost there," Isaac whispers. "Do you?"

"It is hard to say."

"Open up, you fuck." Scott Harley, such a charmer.

Isaac sighs. "I'm glad we waited," he says.

"I am so happy for us." He does not detect the sarcasm. He walks the way we came.

I watch the back door. I estimate the time it would take to clear the distance. I calculate the risk of being caught before I have escaped.

———

EXT. ISAAC'S HOUSE—DAY

I stand flush against the side of the house. My heart races.

Isaac's voice carries through the open kitchen window.

"You'll never guess who's drinking with us." He notices I am gone. "Miles?"

"Miles is here?"

"Miles was here."

"The wet blanket? Here? No way."

"I'm serious."

He will realize I left via the back door. When he does, I am ready to run as fast as my jeans will allow.

"Dude, you're wrecked," Harley says.

"No, he was… He went shopping. The groceries were right there."

A bag of groceries hangs from each hand.

"Wrecked," Harley insists.

I flee.

———

INT. MILES'S BEDROOM—DAY

I sit forward in my desk chair, and my eyes scan from margin to margin. I revise the document, searching for opportunities to add authenticity. Every essay Isaac and I sell starts as a Miles Cooper. This essay is meant to pass for a Brent Rodgers, so I simplify the verbs and split the infinitives.

We sell the best, but the best is relative.

I can hear the vacuum cleaner approaching. Eventually, Dad appears outside my door. He pulls the machine closer with a violent tug of the hose. He is surprised to see me at my desk.

"When did you get in?" he asks. He switches the vacuum off with his toe.

"Not long ago."

He lays the hose down carefully—Mom has warned him about the hardwood floors and he knows I am watching. "That was a short movie."

"The showing was sold out."

"Ah." Dad nods slowly. His eyes drift to the shelves, overstuffed with books and everything that cannot go anywhere else. He takes up a statuette and turns it over in his hand. "How long are you going to keep these?"

There are four statuettes from last year, made to look as much like Oscars as they could without infringing on any copyright. I really like having them there.

"Who are they hurting?" I ask.

"They're dust collectors." He replaces it and glances around the room. I can tell it is not as tidy as he would like.

"Today," I tell him. "As soon as I finish my work."

"Good man."

I look back at the document and *posits* sticks out like a sore thumb. I amend it to *suggests* and then to *says*. *Says* is more Brent Rodgers. We have been selling essays for almost two years. It is this sort of attention to detail that has kept us from getting caught. Without it, I am certain we would have been hauled in to see Mrs. Evans by now.

INT. MRS EVANS'S OFFICE—DAY

As the deputy headmistress of Barton House, Mrs. Evans

deals with two types of students. There are the delin-quents, like Harley. He has been dragged in here so many times his loyalty card is one hole punch away from a free coffee. Then there are the athletic achievers, like Ryan. Mrs. Evans is wild about sports, as are most of Barton House's higher-ups. Her office is decorated with framed photographs, tributes to every student who has ever held a rugby ball.

Harley is here, Ryan is here…and I am here. I have never had her ask to see me before. This is new.

She must know about the essays. It is the only ex-planation for why we are all here at the same time. She has caught Isaac, and recognizing the operation is a so-phisticated one, she is trying to figure out who else is involved. In inviting Ryan and Harley, though, she has betrayed how little she knows.

Isaac and I have prepared for this. He takes the fall. I deny, deny, deny.

Her wrists are reinforced by bracelets. Each movement is a symphony, so she keeps her hands still. She asks us how we are.

"Very well, thanks," I answer.

I wonder how she found out. I doubt it was a client. What they get out of it is linked to how well they keep their silence. Our messaging has been clear: if they tell their friends, their advantage diminishes, because their friends will want in. We do not need word of mouth. We do not want it. It is too risky. All it takes to compro-mise everything is one client telling the wrong person. So we encourage secrecy.

We approach clients, not the other way around. And we only approach the ones we trust to play by our rules.

It could not have been my writing. I am always careful. Somebody must have witnessed a drop. Or Isaac must have bragged.

Mrs. Evans mentions him.

He could have had one too many refreshments, enough to make him think telling one person would not hurt...

Mrs. Evans's features soften. She says he died.

I fall out of myself. I picture us contained within a 16:9 frame sitting opposite her desk: me in the winter uniform, full blazer with pants; Ryan in the summer option, shorts and knee-high socks; Harley in his own custom casual interpretation, a shirt that is slightly untucked but not completely, a top button that is undone but obscured by a tie, and white socks visible only when he sits and his trouser legs ride up. The three of us stare at her, stunned.

"Wait, what?" Harley asks.

INT. CHAPEL—DAY

"Isaac's family may visit in the coming days to collect his belongings from his locker," Mrs. Evans tells the cohort. "If you cross paths, please, display the compassion Barton boys are renowned for."

I peel off my glasses and wipe my eyes. I pause.

My mind catches up with her words.

They are collecting Isaac's belongings. He kept our earnings in his locker. He promised they would be safe there, and I knew if they found the money in his locker and not mine, it would be easier for them to believe he acted alone.

I need to get into his locker.

INT. CORRIDOR—DAY

I tear the red pouch out of Ryan's hands. He fumbles over his words. He is pressing me for details I do not want to give.

I look him in the eyes. "This did not happen."

INT. LIBRARY—DAY

The bottom of my backpack is a bed of crumbs and crumpled paper. I lay the red pouch down and pile everything on top—folders, books. I zip it up and thread my arms through the straps. I usually keep my bag in the cages between the library entrance and the security detectors, where it is closer to most of my classes than it is in my locker, but there is not usually anything in it that is worth stealing.

I peer between the security detectors. Mrs. Lang sits on her high stool at the circulation desk, looking severe. She guards the entrance and chastises any student who dares enter with a bag big enough to smuggle books in.

Ideally, I would spend lunch in the library, sitting cross-legged by the stacks of an ignored genre, where I could go unnoticed and process what has happened. Given my lock is on Isaac's locker, my bag and I are inseparable, at least until I take the money home.

I will have to spend lunch elsewhere.

————

INT. MEETING ROOM—DAY
I sit at a long conference table with the bag still strapped to me. The meeting room across from the library is reserved for staff and supposed to be locked.

There is a laminated poster taped to the wall. The outline of a lady with feathered '80s hair correctly administers CPR on a boy. I think of Isaac.

I wonder softly. What if I had stayed? What if I had been there? What if I had saved him?

My mind pulls on the thread, but I resist. There is nothing on the other side of it that will make me feel any better. My mind pulls harder. I *would* have been there if I had only…

————

BEGIN FLASHBACK:
INT. ISAAC'S KITCHEN—DAY
"You brought a ~~book~~ bottle of vodka to a gathering?" Isaac asks.

"It is a gathering," I say. "What were you expecting? A book? I also brought organic kale chips so Ryan can eat something if he comes."

Isaac says it slowly. "Organic." He mouths it twice more, stretching the O.

I laugh. "You all right?"

Isaac's mouth hangs open, suspended in animation. He shakes it off and blinks at me. *"Hmm?"*

"You seem high."

Isaac beams. "I am very high."

I grab the bottle by the neck and twist off its cap. "In that case, I better catch up!"

I take a long swig. It tastes like whatever vodka tastes like.

The doorbell rings. Isaac bounces on the spot. "Betcha that's Harley," he says.

"Great. I do not hate him in the slightest."

The phone on the kitchen counter vibrates. It distracts Isaac. "Who's that?" he asks.

I reach for the phone.

END FLASHBACK.

———

INT. MEETING ROOM—DAY

Mom's number flashes as the phone vibrates in my hand. She gave it to me on my first day at Barton House. The edges are chipped, there is a crack across the bottom of the screen, and every operating-system update has made it respond a little slower, but I am attached to it. Even more now.

I have had it for exactly as long as I knew Isaac.

The phone stops vibrating. The screen darkens. I place it down.

There is a little conference hub in the center of the table. I drag it closer. A prerecorded female voice tells me to press 0 for external numbers. I do as she says and punch Mom's work number into the pad. The dial tone fills the room, and then Mom's voice, smooth and professional. "Hello, this is Holly."

"Hi, Mom."

She gasps like her heart is torn. The school has notified her. "Miles!"

I preempt the questions. "I am fine."

She does not ask anything. Instead, she offers one loaded "Oh, Miles."

"I am all right."

"Wait… Where are you calling me from?"

"It is a school number."

"Are you in the office?"

I can practically see her sitting at her workstation, wanting to know I am being looked after. Not sitting in an empty meeting room at lunch. "Yeah."

Mom sighs. "Good. That's good. There are people with you?"

"Yes. Mrs. Evans, Mr. Ford." I look around at the vacant chairs.

"Can you put her on?"

"Who?"

"The deputy."

"She is… Uh, I could get her, but she is speaking with Ryan and Harley." I have learned never to say no to Mom—it is easier to make her think she does not need what she wants.

"Right. Of course. She has her hands full. You boys." She exhales into the phone. She is thinking of the others.

I am not. They are on their own.

"I can't believe it. I can't believe it." She is scrambling to be useful. "What can I do? Do you want to catch a cab to my work?"

"No. I am fine."

"Are you sure?"

I am not fine. I am somewhere between numb and broken, but I cannot imagine being in Mom's office, under her constant supervision, will make it any better. At least here, I know where to hide.

"I am sure," I tell her. "Honestly, we are all here. We are all together."

"All right."

"Mrs. Evans is waving me over—I should go."

"Oh. Okay."

"Bye, Mom."

"Love you." There is a weight to it that I have never noticed before, like it is potentially the last time I will hear her say it, or the last chance I will have to say it back.

"Love you too."

Mom does not hang up right away. We sit in each other's silence. It is the comfort before the *click*. When that comes, it is because someone says her name on the other end of the line and she has to go. *Click*. I am alone in another silence, one that feels deeper than the one before the call.

It occurs to me that Isaac and I will never be this close again.

Time is pulling us apart. With every second that passes, the space between us widens. Today, I saw him yesterday. In a few days, it will have been last week. Then, last month. And there is nothing I can do to keep time from wedging more of itself between us. It is inevitable.

I sink forward a little, restrained by the straps of my backpack, and shatter in slow motion.

INT. SCIENCE LAB—DAY

Mr. Barber assigns some pages from our Chemistry textbook, but reading them is more a suggestion than a task. The class is distracted, sitting in clusters, reeling from the news. I have my textbook open to page eighty-nine, as directed. I can feel their eyes on me.

It is Junior Chemistry A's amateur production of *Stares and Whispers*. It has everything: stares, whispers and me, daring to do the assigned work. A play in one act.

I catch morsels.

"…what they think actually happened…"

"…the article says…"

"…yeah, there was a reporter out on the main road at lunch…"

"…interviewed Ex before Mrs. Evans stopped…"

Mr. Barber runs device-free Chemistry classes, but even he spends today with his eyes glued to his phone. In the row ahead, five guys lean into one screen, reading the article about Isaac. It is a regular *Herald Daily* hack job. It pitches Isaac as some bona fide acting prodigy. In truth, he took Drama for the easy A and he was in the film only because I asked.

Point of View is premium award bait. Stylish, gritty, it follows three inner-city teens questioned for the same crime. The screen is permanently split in two. On one side, they narrate their version of events, and on the other, that narration is acted out. The film's ten minutes are the best of hours and hours of raw footage. It is all still sitting on the school server, probably.

Curious, I pull my laptop closer. I exit the *Herald Daily* site and click into the shared drive. The computer struggles with the basic command. Eventually the contents start to load. It is a labyrinth of folders within folders. One click reveals a half-dozen new folders, and in each of those, a half-dozen more. Seven folders deep, I find the one labeled COOPER_FILM. I click it. A long list of video files appears, sorted by date.

I filmed Isaac's narration first. I click ISAAC_01. The frame of the video player appears, then the playback options fill in, and finally, the video. Isaac is in the center of the 16:9 frame. The shot is a medium close-up.

ISAAC looks down at his lap. His ginger mop of hair has grown way past what the school considers acceptable, grazing his collar.

                    ISAAC
        And I'm just there like—

I mute the audio.

Omar has ripped his eyes from his computer. For a second, he thought he heard a dead guy behind him.

I force a smile.

Dylan looks at him. "Man, have you posted anything on Isaac's profile?" he asks.

Omar turns away. "Yeah. It got seventeen likes. Not my best. I might repost it tonight."

"Tag Cara in it and all the North Shore chicks will like it."

I do not know who Cara is or why she controls a faction of girls from the North Shore. She is Isaac's type, powerful in insignificant high-school ways. I only ever heard stories about the girls. I was never allowed to meet them. Isaac said Ryan and Harley made better first impressions.

His lips are moving on my screen.

I pull my earphones out of my pocket in one knotted cluster. I set to work unwinding it as well as I can. I wrangle enough of the cord free to plug into my computer and my ears without having to strain my neck.

MILES kneels behind the camera, offscreen.
RYAN and HARLEY are there too, also offscreen.

           HARLEY (O.S.)
   Tiff's a little weird about you now.

           ISAAC
        (to Harley)
   She's always been weird about me.

           HARLEY (O.S.)

Well, you hook up with her and that
happens. I had to convince her going
out with you isn't what she wants.

        ISAAC
     (to Harley)
What? Are you serious?

        HARLEY (O.S.)
She calls and goes, she wants me to
test the waters, see if you'd want to.

        MILES (O.S.)
Isaac.

        ISAAC
     (to Harley)
And?

        HARLEY (O.S.)
I tell her to close her eyes and
listen to her inner voice—cracks me
up now that I'm saying it—and her
inner voice tells her she doesn't
want Zac, just a boyfriend, and she's
projecting onto the closest guy.

        ISAAC
     (to Harley)
Thanks.

>   HARLEY (O.S.)
> No worries.

>   ISAAC
>   (to Harley)
> Remember to do that with every girl
> you talk to who knows me.

>   MILES (O.S.)
> Isaac.

>   ISAAC
>   (to Miles)
> Hey.

Isaac smirks through time. I whisper, "Hey," right back at him.

————————

INT. STATION PLATFORM—DAY

I wait at the southern end, right where the rear doors of the front car open. Isaac always thought it was pedantic, but it saves me time at Ashfield. Two minutes—that is how long Isaac said it would take anyone to walk the full length of the platform. But it makes sense to board the train where it is best to disembark from. It is efficient.

I check the monitor suspended from the ceiling. There are three minutes until the express, but there is no telling how long it will actually be. Time is flexible down here. Minutes are exaggerated and truncated to ensure that trains always arrive on time.

I hold my computer against my thigh. I have not put it away since I rediscovered the footage. I downloaded all the files from the server before I left.

I check my phone. There are two new emails. The first, to my school account from Anthony Ford.

Miles— I lament not having had a chance to speak with you properly after the...

I close the email without reading further. I can recognize the start of a sales pitch, and I am not buying. I understand the value of counseling, I really do, but it is dangerous at a place like Barton House. Once Mr. Ford starts pulling students from class and singling them out with waves in the corridor, others notice. It brands them. And I do not need more stares and whispers.

And besides, who uses *lament* nowadays?

I check the second email. It lands in the Black Ops inbox. It is from Xavier Jones. He prefers Ex, but that just makes me think everyone dated him at some point.

Are we still good for tomorrow? Ex.

Xavier Jones of *Herald Daily*–article fame wants to know if Isaac dying will affect the delivery of his essay. I want to rage against him for being so tactless, but he does have a point. Am I good for tomorrow? And the tomorrow after that? I have not thought properly about what today means for our operation going forward.

Isaac was the public face. He delivered the product and accepted the payment. As far as anybody knows, it started and ended with Isaac.

This can be my clean break.

Alternatively, I could find someone else to be the public face. Problem is, I do not really like anyone else, let alone trust them. And they would need to be as ethically dubious as Isaac.

I delete the email. The train pulls in and the rear doors of the front car open right in front of me.

———————

INT. TRAIN CAR—DAY
I have the computer on my lap. The world whips past. Isaac is in my ears.

Isaac squints past the camera, at Miles, offscreen.

                    ISAAC
        What's your plan for the weekend?

So like Isaac to have his eyes firmly on the weekend.

                    MILES (O.S.)
        Study.

                    ISAAC
                (aghast)
        Study? It's March. What are you
        studying?

                    MILES (O.S.)
        Can you just say your line?

                    ISAAC
        I'm curious, what is there to study
        one month into the school year?

                    MILES (O.S.)
        Isaac.

                    ISAAC
        What? I'm waiting for you to say,
        "Action!"

                    MILES (O.S.)
        When I say that, Harley just—

                    ISAAC
        He won't.

Harley and Ryan are there too, offscreen.

                    MILES (O.S.)
                (sighs)
        Action.

```
                    HARLEY (O.S.)
          Not getting any!


                    MILES (O.S.)
                 (to Harley)
          That is it. Out.


                    HARLEY (O.S.)
                 (to Miles)
          But I—


                    MILES (O.S.)
                 (to Harley)
          Out.
```

Within his 16:9 frame, Isaac is delighted. He watches what the camera does not capture: me struggling to pull Harley off his seat and drag him to the door.

On the way past, one of us nudges the tripod. The scene within the frame tilts.

```
                    HARLEY (O.S.)
                 (to Isaac)
          Fare ye well!


                    MILES (O.S.)
                 (to Harley)
          Thee. Fare thee well.


                    ISAAC
```

                    (to Harley)
          I miss thee already.

The door shuts.

                    MILES (O.S.)
          Idiot.

                    ISAAC
          Don't be harsh... He's smarter than
          you give him credit for.

                    MILES (O.S.)
          Right.

                    ISAAC
                    (tilting his head)
          Let's be artsy and film it at this
          angle.

Miles tampers with the tripod.

   Isaac blurs as the frame rocks. When it settles, the
angle is even more severe. The autofocus kicks in and
Isaac cocks an eyebrow.

                    MILES (O.S.)
          Damn.

                    ISAAC
          You're not very good at this, are you?

> MILES (O.S.)
Shut up.

> ISAAC
You don't seem to be enjoying it.

> MILES (O.S.)
Let me just—

The clip ends.

I clear my throat and snap the computer shut. Almost at Ashfield anyway.

BEGIN FLASHBACK:
INT. ENGLISH CLASSROOM—DAY

The young-filmmakers program is not about *enjoyment*. When he pitches it, Mr. Mochan says it is about autonomy, creativity and teamwork. On the other side of his midcareer crisis, Mr. Mochan wants to do more than assign and assess essays students have learned by rote—he wants to inspire. He wants us to think outside the box.

For extracurricular credit, the top Sophomore English class is invited to make a short film over the course of three terms, in addition to the syllabus. Like most Barton House invitations, it does not feel like we have a choice. As far as mandatory additional assignments go, it could be worse. This one comes with a film festival, an awards ceremony, an opportunity for Miles Cooper to triumph.

Mr. Mochan wants us in groups of four—quite a task for a class of twenty-five, but his specialty is words, not numbers. While others panic to make their alliances, I stay put. There needs to be a group of five, and I want to make an informed decision. When there are six groups of four, and me, looking back at him, Mr. Mochan catches up. He suggests I join one, but by then, I have decided to work alone.

I will do it all if I join a group, and what is the use in sharing glory?

Mr. Mochan is hesitant, but it does not feel like he has a choice.

INT. ENGLISH CLASSROOM—DAY

Ryan lies across two desks. Isaac looks over his lines for the first time. Harley is here for moral support. I adjust the tripod.

"I think you should do one take with a traffic cone on your head," Harley says. "Just legit don't acknowledge it at all."

"Brilliant," Isaac says.

He is not so much focused on bringing my directorial vision to life as he is on creating the greatest blooper reel.

INT. CHAPEL—NIGHT

I stand at the podium, clutching my fourth statuette of the night. Another Miles Cooper triumph.

Humility always plays well. I thank Isaac, Ryan and Harley, without whose help the film would not have been possible. I dedicate it to them.

END FLASHBACK.

INT. MILES'S BEDROOM—DAY

"Is that you, Miles?" Dad is home early from work. His are slow, deliberate footsteps down the corridor.

I zip the pouch and push it against the back of my wardrobe. I obscure it with a stack of folded T-shirts and Dad appears in the doorway.

"Hey, bud," he says.

"Hi."

He lifts his mouth so his mustache grazes his bottom lip. "How was your afternoon?"

"No one died, so it was a big improvement on my morning."

Dad raps his knuckles on the doorframe. "Ah." He seems a little deflated, like he expected his question to launch a heart-to-heart.

I hesitate. "Thanks for asking, though."

He perks up a bit. "Well, if you need to talk."

"I have your address."

It takes him a moment. "Down the hall." He even points.

I nod. "Yes, Dad."

He asks if I am hungry. Mom is making breakfast for dinner. I realize I missed lunch.

"Sounds good."

EXT. BARTON HOUSE GATES—DAY

There is an art to being invisible.

Mrs. Evans will stand by reception, checking for uniform violations.

I linger just inside the gates, before the stairs up into the building, waiting for an interpretation of the school uniform so abhorrent that she will not see anything else.

A wall of guys with ties askew and untucked shirts cross the Barton House threshold. Their long socks are gathered at their ankles and their shorts are streaked with mud. They have been playing rugby in the park.

I let them climb the stairs. I cannot be right behind them or Mrs. Evans will see me too. The space between us equals time, time for Mrs. Evans to spot them, call them over, chastise them, insist they tidy themselves.

Head down, I start up the stairs.

INT. MR. FORD'S OFFICE—DAY

I am certain school policy dictates that Mr. Ford is unavoidable in situations like mine, so I get my visit over with before first period. I anticipate he will ask me how I am feeling, and he does.

I tell him, "I have felt like this before." I pause, for effect. "It is not grief, no, I have never lost anyone close to me before, but I have felt *this*, if that makes sense?" I feign doubt in myself so the speech seems less rehearsed. He nods at me like his feedback will have any impact on what is coming next.

"It was my final exam for Freshman English. I thought I was so clever. I had an essay I learned by heart, three perfect paragraphs I could rework to fit any question. I opened the exam booklet, and those three perfect paragraphs did not fit *that* question. I glanced around the exam hall, and everyone else was writing. I was paralyzed by fear. But I had to try. First, I stalled. I reworded the question as a statement, hoping that once I was done, there would be another sentence to back it up. And there was. The words started to flow. The more I wrote, the easier it became, and before long, I had plucked an essay out of nowhere." I flash a smile. "It worked out in the end."

I shift in my seat. "This is the same, I guess. I prepared for a world with Isaac in it. He was a perfect paragraph in the essay of my life." I regret it as soon as I say it. It feels too corny, but it hits the right note with Mr. Ford. I continue, "It is a shock, and I cannot say for certain if the new essay will be better or worse. It will be different, but I have to answer the question I have been given. I have to try."

Mr. Ford nods sagely. "You know, what's always struck me about you is your maturity," he says. "Learning from life's challenges, that's maturity."

"Oh, thank you, sir."

I have never prepared poorly for an exam in my life.

INT. CORRIDOR—DAY

At break, I try the door to the meeting room I sat in yesterday. It is locked.

"Damn," I mutter.

INT. LIBRARY STUDY ROOM—DAY

The door clicks shut behind me. Jamie looks up from the newspaper.

"Hey," he says.

"Hello."

I would rather a room to myself, but the library is especially busy today, so I have to make do with sharing. Jamie Cummins and I started at Barton House the same time. I remember sitting next to him at seventh-grade orientation. They must have orientated him one way and me another, because our paths have hardly intersected since.

I walk to the end of the room, which sounds farther than the six feet it actually is. I set my computer down on the table and pull back the top. The screen blinks to life. The folder of film footage is open, ready for my next selection. Beyond the computer, Jamie watches me with wide green eyes.

"How are you?" His voice drips with fascination.

"I am good."

Jamie does not turn away. I think he expected a bleaker

answer. I plug one earphone in and raise the other. It is just shy of my ear when he says, "Ryan isn't good. He seems pretty beat, and no one's seen Harley. He didn't stay at the boardinghouse last night. Guys are saying he went on a bender."

Ah, Harley's world-famous benders. He drinks for one day but disappears for two because the myth maketh the man.

I insert the second earphone and exit the conversation. I select a file. The video player struggles to load and then Isaac's laughter explodes from my computer's speakers.

Isaac scratches his nostril with his thumb.

            ISAAC
      So what exactly is my motivation in
      this sce—?

I pause the clip too late. Jamie has recognized Isaac's voice. I did not plug the earphones into the computer. Stupid. Stupid.

Jamie chews on the inside of one cheek. "What are you watching?" he asks.

INT. CORRIDOR—DAY
I try the meeting room again at lunch. Still locked.

INT. ANOTHER CORRIDOR—DAY

I press my head against the glass door of the darkened room.

The computer lab is a relic of the recent past before the one-to-one laptop initiative. The space has been abandoned long enough to be forgotten, but not long enough to be refurbished into someplace useful.

It is perfect.

Mr. Tan is mediating a crisis between two eighth graders. I interject to ask him to open the door. Remaining absorbed by the crisis, he works his key off the ring and hands it to me. I walk to the door and unlock it, and when I turn back, he is gone. The crisis has led him farther down the corridor.

"Fair enough." I pocket the key.

INT. COMPUTER LAB—DAY

Computers line all four walls. I gravitate toward the one reserved for teachers. It is hooked up to the projector. When I get it all working, Isaac is no longer contained to a tiny computer screen but projected three feet tall. I drag a chair into the center of the room and sit in the dark. It is like my own private cinema.

The wall glows, the projected colors bounce and Isaac washes over me. He consults the script in his lap, and the red of his hair tints the sleeve of my shirt. He looks up; our gazes meet.

Isaac blinks. He is watching Miles, offscreen.

                    ISAAC
How long will it take you to edit this?

                    MILES (O.S.)
Ages.

                    ISAAC
Why?

                    MILES (O.S.)
I have to cut out stuff like this.

                    ISAAC
Was that a hint?

                    MILES (O.S.)
Maybe.

                    ISAAC
Do I talk too much?

                    MILES (O.S.)
Definitely.

I cannot disagree more. I could listen to him forever. I am disappointed when Isaac actually starts reciting his lines.

Last year, I had to edit out all the filler between takes. Now the filler is all I want.

INT. MILES'S LIVING ROOM—NIGHT

When I tell Mom I do not have any homework, she insists I not retreat to my room after dinner. Whatever I will do in there, I can do on the couch, she says, betraying a severe lack of understanding of how teenage boys like to spend their free time. It is obvious she is trying to be supportive. I want to assure her that I am fine. I have Isaac's footage and I do not need supporting.

But I would prefer to keep the footage secret, so I sit on the couch. She takes the armchair. We keep two books under the coffee table for quiet moments. When one is finished, it is replaced. Mom hands me the paperback. I turn to the dog-eared page. She handles the hardcover on molecular biology with more care.

"Do you understand any of that?" I ask.

She uses a male underwear model cut out of a catalog as a bookmark. "Dion will help me through." She calls him Dion. I do not know how Dad feels about that.

I read the first line of the page twice. So much has happened since I last put the book down, it all feels foreign to me. I try the line a third time and my phone's notification light blinks.

I unlock the screen, revealing a new Black Ops email from Michael Wilson. It is brief.

Drama wasn't the same without you, man.

I have not taken Drama since it was mandatory in eighth grade.

Oh, *you*.

Michael is talking to Isaac. That makes sense. As far as any client knows, Isaac answered the emails.

Drama wasn't the same without you, man.

My eyes water before I realize it has upset me.

INT. CORRIDOR—DAY

The seniors line both sides of the corridor. A kid half their height lingers just out of their reach, hesitant. They chant, "Run it! Run it!"

Barton House has what Mrs. Evans calls a negative corridor culture—in the five minutes between periods, narrow arteries struggle to pump hundreds of students from one class to the next, and that brings out the worst in human nature. Leave a senior class waiting long enough outside their room and they will form a gauntlet. They usually target younger students, but I am built like a sheet of cardboard.

I step into the gauntlet with a viselike grip on my books.

There are two shoves, then a teacher's "Hey!" cuts through the air and the seniors snap back against the wall. I can now see past them, and Michael Wilson walking toward me.

I call his name.

His brow creases. "Hi?"

Ah. He does not know he emailed me. I try to recover. "You take Modern History, right?"

Michael shakes his head.

I force a short laugh. "Why did I think you did?"

He shrugs and says he is running late.

"Yeah, no, right, bye." He passes and I berate myself. Stupid. Stupid.

INT. COMPUTER LAB—DAY

I have Isaac's profile projected on the wall and the cordless mouse on my thigh.

He lives in a box in the top corner, reflected in his bathroom mirror. His orange hair is coiffed, his jawline is pronounced and he has rolled up his sleeves to accentuate his biceps. He took the photo himself. I would be mortified if I had left that digital footprint, but he does not seem bothered.

I scroll down and try to absorb the posts. Everybody is competing for likes.

I close the browser and unwrap my sandwich.

INT. MILES'S KITCHEN—DAY

Mom overdoes breakfast. Bacon, eggs, mushrooms, sliced avocado and a stack of pancakes on the side. It is the sort of decadence that precedes French revolutions, not

Thursdays. Any hope of ducking out with a piece of toast in my mouth and a wave is dashed.

"You have time," Mom says, preempting my excuse. "Your father can drop you at the station."

Dad's face says they have not discussed this. Mom pulls up a chair beside him and waits for me to join them. I peel off my backpack and take the free seat.

Mom eats all the mushrooms she has served herself, then starts to fork them off Dad's plate. "Gerard is okay with me taking a half day," she says.

She wants to come to the funeral. I tell her no one else's parents are going to be there.

"Ryan's will be."

"But she is a teacher."

She goes for Dad's last mushroom, and he blocks her with his fork. I twist my plate so that my mushrooms are closest to her. She makes a start on those. "Are you certain you'll be fine?"

———

INT. SCIENCE LAB—DAY
Mr. Barber faces the whiteboard. He is talking the class through last night's homework but he has hit a roadblock. He checks the page in his hand and then adjusts what he has written on the board.

ISAAC
Have you thought about zombie vampires?

                MILES (O.S.)

What about them?

                ISAAC

Let's put them in the movie.

                MILES (O.S.)
        (beat)
Really?

                ISAAC

Yeah, why not?

                MILES (O.S.)

How would it even work? Would they
be vampires first who then became
zombies, or were they zombies who
were then bitten by vampires?

                ISAAC

That's the film!

                MILES (O.S.)
        (beat)
No.

It works like an IV drip of memory. My computer
sits to one side, propped open just enough to keep from
hibernating. The cord snakes from the audio jack, up

under my blazer and out my left sleeve. The bud sits in
my palm, pressed against my head.

> ISAAC
> Okay, then. What if we shoot one
> scene completely hammered?

I can hear Isaac's smile. It softens his words, but they
have a different meaning now. Between his mouth and my
ears, they pass through everything that has happened since.

> ISAAC
> (continuing)
> It won't tank the film—we'll make
> sure it isn't obvious, so at the
> screening, the top brass of the
> school will watch it and not realize
> they've just seen us wasted.

It is all I can do not to shatter while Isaac speaks. That
would be excellent for my social standing, bursting at the
seams with sadness in the middle of Chemistry.

> ISAAC
> (continuing)
> What? *No bueno?* Harley thinks it's a
> good idea.

I snap the laptop shut and Isaac is quiet. Mr. Barber is
searching the whiteboard for his error. I check my work and
identify where our calculations diverge. I raise my hand.

"The equation is imbalanced," I tell him.

Mr. Barber checks over his shoulder. "It is?"

"Yes. There should be two molecules on the right instead of one."

He makes the adjustment. "So there should."

"Also, may I go to the bathroom?"

––––––––––

INT. BATHROOM—DAY

I stare at my reflection. Leaning on my hand in class has flattened a patch of hair by my ear. I produce a comb from my top blazer pocket and try to tease some volume into it.

I remember a character doing something similar before their own friend's funeral.

Last year, Mr. Mochan encouraged us to immerse ourselves in visual stories. We could not be young filmmakers without an intimate understanding of the medium. I probably took it too far, consuming hours of video, mostly television. I started to notice the repetitions. When someone dies on television, there is an arc to it. Characters grieve, there is lots of watching their own reflections, lots of contemplation, and in the episodes that follow the funeral, they begin to embrace life without the deceased and meet the new kid who looks strangely like the person who has just died. After a few episodes, the new character goes from existing on the show's fringes to featuring in its opening credits.

That is largely how it goes. Largely, not always. Sometimes, a character might grieve, do everything they are supposed to, like contemplate opposite their own reflection, but when they try to rebuild their life, they falter. They are redefined by their persistent sadness, and they are never quite the same.

I run the comb through my hair.

That will not be me, will it?

No. I have the footage. I am fine. I am fine.

The door swings open. Ryan enters shoulder first. His tie hangs unmade around his neck. He is surprised to see me standing here.

We exchange greetings and the occasional glance. He struggles to tie a knot. I can see him bouncing back after this. Swimming is everything to him. Two episodes and he will be fine. I am sure of it.

And I have the footage. I am fine. I am...not sure of it.

"Do you ever worry about getting depression?" I ask Ryan.

INT. CORRIDOR—DAY

I hesitate. The rest of my class files into the chapel. Through the doorway, past the adults exchanging solemn looks, I see the coffin. Isaac's photograph rises from a bed of flowers.

I fall out of myself. I picture the extreme close-up of my mouth as my breathing wavers, and then the mid shot from my right side that reveals the corridor and stream of students walking toward the chapel.

I step back. Omar asks me where I am going.

INT. COMPUTER LAB—DAY
I steady my trembling hand and select ISAAC_01. I look
to the wall and Isaac fills it.

Isaac looks down at his lap.

                    ISAAC
          And I'm just there like, "What are
          you doing?"

I exhale. Isaac is alive.
Isaac is alive.

INT. COMPUTER LAB—DAY
SUPERIMPOSE: TWO WEEKS LATER
I pause the footage. Isaac is blurred midmotion. I jump
forward a few frames until he is in focus. Perfect.

Isaac smiles.

"So, what is for lunch today?" I ask for him. It is penne
drenched in some kind of secret sauce. I pop open the
plastic container and catch a whiff. "Yes. You are not
missing much, to be honest. Anyway, in English..." I
shovel some penne out and taste it. "Actually, revising
my verdict. This is not half-bad."

`Isaac smiles.`

If I had to guess, I would say I have eight or so hours of Isaac footage. It might seem like a lot, but in the context of how many hours I have to fill in a week, it is not much. I have to pace myself. I have to pause pretty regularly. We have a chat. Well, I chat and Isaac smiles. I like it.

"So, English…"

————

INT. MILES'S LIVING ROOM—NIGHT
I slide my book back under the coffee table and push up off the lounge. On my way past her, Mom asks, "How are the boys?"

"Good. We are talking a lot."

"That's good."

————

INT. COMPUTER LAB—DAY
"I got a Chemistry assignment back. I came first in the class by half a grade."

`Isaac smiles.`

————

INT. CORRIDOR—DAY
"Miles!"

I stop and Michael quickens his pace to catch up.

"Hey." He rolls his neck a weird way and it cracks. "We were talking in Drama about your movie from last year. Do you still have it?" He leans in like it is a secret. "The one with Isaac in it?"

"Um."

I have never contemplated showing *Point of View* again. It was made for one night and one very specific audience. Its success at the festival had less to do with the film and more to do with the jury and what I knew about each juror. Brother Mitchell, a man of faith, he was especially moved by the religious themes. Ms. Thomson, a mother, she was pleased to see her son in such a prominent role. Mrs. Herrera, a late addition to the jury, she saw her culture reflected in Harley, who I added to the film at the eleventh hour and had speak in a Spanish accent.

"I reckon it'd be neat," Michael says, "just to see him again."

"I am not sure…"

"Tons of people would want to see it."

INT. COMPUTER LAB—DAY

I do not expect many people to show up. The room gradually fills, and twenty minutes into lunch, Michael closes the door and gives me a thumbs-up. Thirty-three people. We have run out of chairs. I had not anticipated a crowd. I had expected Ryan, though. Perhaps Michael thought I would invite him.

I still have the speech memorized, the one I introduced

Point of View with at the festival, but that was more about appeasing the jurors ("This film features positive representations of people of color, religion and Ryan!") than anything else. I stand in front of thirty-three people and realize this is not about *Point of View.*

This is about Isaac.

"Here it is." I nod and step back.

When he realizes that is the extent of my introduction, Michael dims the lights.

I start the film.

When Isaac first appears on-screen, there are gasps. At some point, I stop watching the projection and watch the others instead.

They stare wide-eyed, enraptured. His narration shots are composed like the rest, but they feel strikingly different. He has a presence on-screen, a charisma death has intensified. His smile is otherworldly.

They look past all the jury-appeasing cleverness and they see Isaac.

Point of View is not Miles Cooper's triumph anymore; it is Isaac Roberts's final starring role.

INT. MILES'S LIVING ROOM—NIGHT

My phone whistles a notification. Mom looks up from her book. Her gaze burns. I do not check my phone until she turns away. It is a new Black Ops email from Michael.

We had a screening of your movie today, man. It was something. All the Drama kids came. Miss you, and not just because I have this piece of shit essay due and could do with a hand. Hope you're rocking it up there.

Goose bumps prick my forearm.

I could help him. All I would need to do is email an essay. There would be no need to do it in person, because I would not be doing it for money. The problem is, it would be too easy to trace back to me. Michael would wonder who wrote it, and who else would write an essay he did not have to?

No, if I were to do it, I would need to deliver it in a way that pinned it on someone else…

———

INT. AQUATIC-CENTER CHANGE ROOM—DAY

I emerge from the cubicle when I am certain all the swimmers are gone.

I find Ryan's bag in one corner. THOMSON is written in Wite-Out beneath the top zipper. I slide the envelope underneath and retreat to the cubicle.

I sit on the lowered lid and wait. The task was not particularly difficult. I found the details on the English department intranet. It was a close textual analysis. We had done something similar, so I could lift whole lines from mine. I added spelling mistakes and syntactical quirks, though, for authenticity.

Someone enters the change room at half past seven. Michael is on time. The footsteps circle as he searches for Ryan's bag. He finds it. He unzips it. I told him the envelope was *under* the bag. He recognizes his error. He zips it up. I strain to hear what he is doing. After a minute, he leaves.

I count to ten and let myself out. I check underneath Ryan's bag. The envelope is still there. I check inside.

Michael has left a fifty-dollar bill.

All I wanted to do was make his life without Isaac a little easier. I had not expected payment, but I am not going to complain about an extra fifty dollars. I pocket it.

———

INT. COMPUTER LAB—DAY
I reread Isaac's *Herald Daily* article.

I would give the world to be mentioned in it once.

———

INT. COMPUTER LAB—DAY
I bite into my sandwich as ISAAC_13 begins to play. It is the final solo Isaac file.

```
Isaac cleans his teeth with his tongue and
bares his grin at Miles, offscreen.

                    ISAAC
        Anything?

                    MILES (O.S.)
        All clear.
```

I cringe. I hate hearing my recorded voice.

                    MILES (O.S.)
               (continuing)
          And go.

Isaac shifts in his seat and clears his
throat. He shifts some more.

                    MILES (O.S.)
               (continuing)
          Sometime this year.

                    ISAAC
               (smirking)
          I have a process.

                    MILES (O.S.)
          Hurry it up, Brando.

                    ISAAC
               (still smirking)
          "Well, sir, I just really think—"

                    MILES (O.S.)
          Can you say it without the smirk?

I lean closer.

Isaac's smirk fades.

                    ISAAC
                 (deadpans)
         Hi. I'm not allowed to show any real
         emotion in this piece.

                    MILES (O.S.)
         Isaac!

Isaac laughs. He applauds himself.

                    ISAAC
         You've gotta admit that was pretty
         funny.

                    MILES (O.S.)
         Yes. Gold star.

Isaac shifts in his seat again. He begins to
chew on the inside of one cheek.

                    MILES (O.S.)
                 (continuing)
         Isaac?

Isaac pops open his mouth to stop chewing.
His gaze is vacant.

                    ISAAC
         Yeah?

                    MILES (O.S.)
          Can I ask you something? And you
          will be honest with me?

Isaac nods.

                    MILES (O.S.)
                (continuing)
          Are you on something?

Isaac scoffs.

                    ISAAC
          It's Friday afternoon, isn't it?

                    MILES (O.S.)
          Is that a yes?

Isaac laughs again.

                    ISAAC
          It's pretty funny.

                    MILES (O.S.)
          Stop saying that. It is not funny.
          I ask you to do this one thing, and
          you show up stoned!

                    ISAAC
          I'm not stoned.

> MILES (O.S.)

Forgive me if I do not know the correct terminology, Isaac.

> ISAAC

Annoying when people correct you,
isn't it?

> MILES (O.S.)
>   (beat)

All I need is ten minutes, two if
you take it seriously and just say
the line.

> ISAAC

All *you* need. This is all you. Your
movie. Your glory. You do it yourself.

Isaac stands up.

> MILES (O.S.)

Very funny. Come on, sit down…

There is a cut, and then:

Miles sits in the seat. His eyes are bloodshot.
He smiles feebly.

> MILES

I guess it is just you and me now.

I look into my own eyes. I remember that feeling.

INT. MILES'S BEDROOM—NIGHT

I sit on the edge of my bed and watch the four statuettes standing on the top shelf—Best Film, Best Director, Best Script and Best Editor. From the moment Mr. Mochan pitched the festival idea to the night of the festival itself, I worked for those four statuettes. I lived and breathed that film. And I triumphed.

BEGIN FLASHBACK:
INT. CHAPEL—NIGHT

I stand at the podium, clutching my fourth statuette of the night.

"And thank you to Isaac, Ryan and Harley," I say, "without whose help this film would not have been possible."

I see their three seats in the back row are empty. They must have ducked out between awards.

"I dedicate this to them," I say anyway.
END FLASHBACK.

INT. MILES'S BEDROOM—NIGHT

Maybe *triumphed* is the wrong word. The more time passes, the less it feels like triumph.

Maybe I should have let Isaac film a scene with a traffic cone on his head, and written in zombie vampires, and acted drunk in one scene.

Maybe then it would have been different. Maybe Isaac would not have shown up under the influence. Maybe he would have stayed for the final award. Maybe I would have featured in his *Herald Daily* article.

Maybe I would not be here, after weeks of watching footage, wondering if he and I really were friends.

"Isaac?" I ask out loud. "Were we actually friends?"

In the absence of an answer, my eyes drift to the floor. My laptop charges at my feet. I pull it up onto the bed and pull back the screen. I navigate to the folder of raw footage. My instinct is to revisit one of his solo clips. I reconsider and select ACTION_01. I have no idea what it is.

The vision is shaky—I am holding the camera in my hands.

```
Ryan and Harley prepare for their fight scene.
Ryan grips his foot and pulls it back, stretch-
ing his quadriceps. Harley sips an energy drink.


              HARLEY
     I don't get how this is going to
     make any sense. Do they just start
     fighting in the middle of—?
```

I stop the clip. Isaac was away that day. I select DIALOGUE_01. My heart skips a beat when I see Isaac

standing on the edge of the frame. He blurs in and out
of focus.

Isaac leans against the wall, exasperated.
Miles is offscreen.

> ISAAC
> Wouldn't it be easier if the others
> were here?

> MILES (O.S.)
> No.

> ISAAC
> Such venom!

I remember the plan. I would get Isaac in focus, then
step into frame and act out the scene. I did not need the
others. We could do it on our own.

> MILES (O.S.)
> Not venomous. I have just accepted
> the fact that I should have written
> a script that required fewer actors.

> ISAAC
> That's venomous. They're my friends.

I can see Isaac clearly now.

                    MILES (O.S.)
          Right. I have it. Stay still.

                    ISAAC
          Staying still.

Miles steps into frame, tucking in his shirt.
He crouches down to place the script at their
feet.

                    MILES
          I honestly cannot fathom how one
          person can be friends with the three
          of us.

                    ISAAC
          If I wanted to be friends with my-
          self, I'd invest in mirrors.

                    MILES
          But we are incompatibly different.

                    ISAAC
          How do I explain this? You're a
          nerd—you play Pokémon, right?

                    MILES
          Yes, I— Wait, I am not a nerd.

                    ISAAC
          Really?

Miles opens his mouth to rebut, but no words come out.

                    ISAAC
                (continuing)
      Well, you know there's animals?

                    MILES
      Pocket Monsters.

                    ISAAC
      See? Nerd. Anyway, you have your
      party of monsters and they fight
      other parties. There's strategy to
      it. You don't win because you have
      six of the same type. You need to
      have a varied group so that what-
      ever someone throws at you, you're
      covered.

                    MILES
      And what? We are your Pokémon?

                    ISAAC
      Yes. The swimmer, the rebel and the
      nerd.

                    MILES
      And what does that make you?

```
                    ISAAC
        The guy with the best team.

Miles smiles. He takes it as a compliment.
```

I do not take it as a compliment now. I was not a friend; I served a function. I was a sidekick, a bit player in Isaac's life. And now that he is gone, what does that make me?

INT. COMPUTER LAB—DAY
I find I doubt our friendship less when I pause the footage.

```
Isaac smiles.
```

There is something so much better about an image that cannot tell me anything I do not want to hear.

"I know it is still more than a year off," I tell Isaac, "but I have started to think about what I want to study next year. I was considering international studies. I think I could be really good at it."

```
Isaac smiles.
```

INT. AQUATIC-CENTER CHANGE ROOM—DAY
SUPERIMPOSE: SOME TIME PASSES
I slide the envelope marked *LAST ONE* underneath the bag marked *THOMSON*.

INT. AQUATIC-CENTER CHANGE ROOM—LATER
SUPERIMPOSE: SOME MORE TIME PASSES
I slide the envelope marked *SERIOUSLY THIS IS IT,*
I AM DEAD underneath the bag marked *THOMSON.*

INT. CORRIDOR—DAY
A seventh grade kid stands with our Modern History
class. He is swimming in his shirt. He asks Omar something, and Omar points over to me.

INT. MS. THOMSON'S OFFICE—MORNING
I linger in the doorway. "Miss?"

Without looking over, she asks me to take one of the
two seats facing her desk. I wonder if her tone is frosty
or if I am just imagining it. There is a bevy of reasons
why a department head might summon me to her office. It does not mean I have been caught. I am careful.
I always add authenticity.

I sit.

"How was the aide?" She means the seventh-grade
helper who fetched me.

"He was good."

"He is one of the good ones." Her eyes twitch. "I
thought you were one of the good ones."

All right. Maybe I did not add enough authenticity. I swallow hard and keep my voice steady. "Pardon?"

She removes her glasses and looks me square in the eyes. "Is my son selling essays that you write?"

I keep still. "No."

That makes her smile. "You're an intelligent young man, Miles. I had hoped you wouldn't make me jump through these hoops."

"What hoops, miss?"

"I know you and Ryan—"

"I am sorry, but I do not really have much to do with Ryan."

"You do understand that I'm his mother, and when he goes to your house, he tells me?"

"He comes to my house?" Ryan has never visited, ever.

She inhales sharply. "Right. I am going to continue my work. You sit tight, think awhile, weigh your options. When you recognize that you have been caught, we can have a chat about what you've done." Her eyes widen.

"No!"

"No?"

Ms. Thomson picks up her phone and dials a number. She looks through the glass panel separating her from the other English staff. Mr. Morgan answers his phone.

"Hank, could you send in the student aide? I need him to fetch my son."

———

INT. CORRIDOR—DAY

Ryan is sour about me using him as a cover. To be accurate, I only used his bag as a cover. His involvement was loosely inferred, at most, but he feels I owe him.

"Tell me what you do at lunch," he says.

I do not understand why he wants to know. He has never shown more than a passing interest in me.

———————

INT. COMPUTER LAB—DAY

When Ryan arrives, I am still of two minds about actually showing him the raw footage. The time I spend in here, it is just ours—Isaac's and mine. Letting Ryan in changes that.

But the time I spend in here, how good is it? How good is what Isaac and I have now? I talk to a frozen frame, because when I unpause the footage, he disappoints me, upsets me, angers me. His faults are on display, but even then, I still miss him.

Ryan must miss Isaac too. Knowing that, I cannot keep the footage from him.

I watch him watch Isaac, the way his breathing changes when he sees him. At one point, he inhales sharply. "Shit, I'm getting goose bumps." He points to his arm. "It's like he's here."

"Yeah," I mutter.

I miss feeling like that when I watched Isaac.

I watch him now and it just hurts. He collected us: the swimmer, the rebel and the nerd. He was the hero, we were his sidekicks. Ryan and Harley, they have swimming and rebelling—they can become their own heroes.

But me? What is the nerd to do but study us, revising our history, over and over?

I explain it to Ryan like a television show. The young-filmmakers program took my brain and realigned it. I fall out of myself and live my experiences as scenes. When I consider my life, I picture the season-long character arc. I do not tell him that, though. I only say it feels like the main actor of the show we are on has left to pursue a movie career.

It is odd—after so much time in here with Isaac, I have forgotten how it feels to have someone talk back.

There is a weight to each of Ryan's replies.

I consider asking him what I have spent countless hours asking myself and asking Isaac. There is no opportunity to until he shakes my hand and a silence settles in the lab.

"Question," I say, more to build up the courage to ask it than anything else. "Were Isaac and I actually friends?"

The lines on his forehead deepen. "What are you on about?"

I rephrase the question. "Did Isaac like me?"

"Yes." His answer is emphatic.

"Then why was he so mean?"

"Oh. In the footage?" I nod and Ryan brushes it off. "You were stressed, and it was funny to mess with you."

"It was not funny for me."

"It was really funny for us." He grins until he realizes he has misjudged the audience and winds it back. "Sorry."

"I know it is not really him," I explain. "Footage is made of samples of the light bouncing off him, assembled together to give the illusion of movement, with recorded

audio running underneath. But it feels so real." My eyes
water. I blink hard. My voice cracks when I continue.
"I know the video is the moment without its context. I
know filming took nine months, and I know I only have
twenty-one hours of footage, and I know I cannot judge
nine months from twenty-one hours, but what I feel over-
powers what I know. It is not an illusion. He lives, he
breathes, he speaks, and when I watch him, he tells me
he hates me."

"Man..."

I wipe my eyes with the back of my hand. I can feel
him pitying me. I must look so stupid.

"You're overthinking it," Ryan says, leaning in. "He
helped with your film. You said it yourself. It took twenty-
one hours of filming, and he was there for most of it. Would
he really have given up that much time if he hated you?"

"He wanted the blooper reel."

"You wouldn't have asked him to help if you thought
he hated you."

That is not entirely true. I always felt my link to Isaac
was the most tenuous. He, Harley and Ryan had gatherings. When Isaac proposed we sell essays and came to
me with a plan that would see him assume all the risk
for a nominal fee, I agreed despite my reservations, because it was something that would bind us. Yes, the film
was largely a quest for personal glory, but it was also an
opportunity to strengthen our bond.

I asked him to help with the film because I doubted us.

I clear my throat. "You are right," I tell him.

INT. MILES'S LIVING ROOM—NIGHT

The paperback is open facedown in my lap. I have my phone out. The conversation with Ryan is empty. My fingers hover over the keypad.

I can see Mom in my peripheries. She bends Dion's head back and gasps when the tear worsens. "I think it's time to retire our good friend Dion," she says with a heavy heart.

"Maybe you could use a photograph of your husband as a bookmark?" Dad suggests from the kitchen.

"No." Mom tilts her head to one side. "Do they still sell firefighter calendars? It would be sturdier material."

"And larger," Dad says.

"Much."

I type, Hi.

INT. COMPUTER LAB—DAY

"Ryan was just in here. I showed him a clip of you two. His face lit up."

Isaac smiles.

"We have been texting, him and I. That is not to say that we are shooting rapid-fire messages back and forth, but we are texting."

Isaac smiles.

"I have not decided whether it is good or bad. It is new. That is all it is at the moment." My phone vibrates in my lap. "Oh! This is him."

I check the text.

RYAN

Harley's back.

Seeing his name again makes my skin crawl. Harley's sole contribution to society is bestowing nicknames upon people. I guess that is why we never clicked. Cooper Adams is already Coops, and he has no idea what to do with Miles.

ME

Are you kidding?

I hope he is.

INT. CORRIDOR—DAY

He is not kidding.

Harley wastes no time making his presence felt. He starts a photographic tribute on Isaac's locker. All it takes is for Ryan to add one and the locker becomes a monument to Isaac, plastered in photos. Guys spend their free periods printing off and adding their photos with him.

I met Isaac on the first day of seventh grade, and since then, we never took a photo together. Did we think we had more time? Did we never have a moment we thought warranted preserving? Did Isaac just not want one with me?

My eyes linger on Harley's photo in the center covered by the corners of the others that have been added since. He and Isaac are standing on a Sydney street. I know for a fact Isaac hated being dragged into the city on weekends, a bus and a train and too much effort, but looking at the photo, no one would realize. Isaac is beaming—they both are. They look so happy.

"He looks so happy, doesn't he?" Omar asks, edging past me to tape his photo to the growing tribute.

"Photos are just lies," I say flatly. "We pose, someone tells us to smile."

Omar does not respond. I think I wanted to hurt him. I wanted him to doubt what he had with Isaac as much as I doubt what I had.

Every single photo on that locker says the same thing: "We were best friends." Each one presents its own reality, and in it, Isaac and Harley, Ryan, Omar, whoever, were inseparable.

I do not have that. I have the footage. That says something else entirely.

———

INT. MODERN HISTORY CLASSROOM—DAY
Ryan leans over the space where Isaac used to sit and whispers, "Harley wants to catch up, the three of us, after school today."

"The three of us?"

"Okay, me and him, but you should come."

I open my mouth to reject the offer, but my realigned brain considers the arc. Ours is unfinished. There is so much that has gone unsaid.

Isaac was never perfect, but there was more to him before Harley arrived. Back then, I took the bad because there was so much good in him. He would not show it often, but he would show it. He was my best friend. And Harley took his shell and made a monster.

He needs to be told as much.

It will be our ending. The three of us have walked mostly diverging paths since Isaac died. Harley, Ryan and I, the sidekicks, will come together one last time. We will resolve everything. Then the camera will slowly pull away and the series will fade to black.

It will be our series finale.

"All right," I tell him.

"Meaning you'll come?"

I nod. "After Squad?"

"I don't have Squad tonight." Ryan looks down at his work. I see something in his eyes, but I do not know what.

INT. CAFÉ—DAY

When Harley sinks into the vacant chair, my smile evaporates.

It is the first time I have seen him in months. In person, anyway. I have seen more than enough footage of him. The worst parts rise to the top of my mind and play like a greatest-hits collection of his garbage humanity.

When he invites me to speak, it is hard to stop.

Every thought that has occurred to me while reviewing the footage spills out. He was a terrible influence, selfish. He goaded Isaac to be his absolute worst. He did not care if Isaac overdid it, so long as he still had a place to crash on the weekends.

I tell him, and he does not go down quietly. We trade barbs.

Ryan intervenes eventually, when we have scarred each other enough. "Christ," he says. He insists we break bread, but the café is out of bread, so we settle for breaking one croissant.

The waiter eyes us strangely.

Ryan nods. "With three plates."

We sit around the table and Ryan awkwardly breaks apart a tiny croissant with his fingers. It is a powerful final image.

I wait for the fade to black. It does not come.

"Want to keep this party going?" Harley asks.

I hesitate. "Actually, I have lots to do."

"We would love to," Ryan answers for me.

It seems our ending is elsewhere.

INT. DINING HALL—NIGHT

Barton House hosts social dinners with the boarders of our sister school. Harley sneaks us in as expertly as he can manage. (We are spotted almost immediately.) He introduces us to his friend Jacqueline, who seems lovely, but I doubt her as a judge of character. The night is neither a failure nor a success; it is a pass. And as it passes, I cannot help but feel like our ability to end is slipping further and further away...

When the younger students begin to clear the plates, Mr. Collins does the rounds to encourage those who do not live here to return to where they do.

Harley hugs Jacqueline. "Good night, lady," he says, looking at me.

An artful dig. Definitely seventh-grade level, which is more than I tend to expect from him.

I must not hide my disdain well, because Ryan mutters, "Don't. He's making an effort."

That is how low our standards are for Harley. He invited us to a dinner he had no authority to invite us to. That is "making an effort."

Harley says goodbye to Ryan with a handshake. Ryan reciprocates with, "I'm bursting. Where's the bathroom?" Harley gives him directions.

That leaves Harley and me in the middle of the dining hall.

"I guess I'll see you tomorrow?"

I opt for honesty. "No."

"Huh?"

"This is our series finale, Harley."

"Our what?"

I sigh. I had hoped he would understand the metaphor, to save me explaining it. I lucked out with Ryan. His mom is head of English. Metaphors are in his genes.

Harley, though… I doubt he has ever got anything right on an English paper besides his name.

"There comes a time when a television show runs its course and exhausts all of its plotlines, and there is no justifiable reason for the characters to still hang around each other. This is our time, Harley."

He shrugs. "Whatever."

———————

INT. MILES'S BEDROOM—NIGHT

I sit on the edge of my bed and loosen my tie. My eyelids feel like they have weights tied to them. I do not think I have ever been out so late on a school night, although, I doubt it really counts considering I was at a Barton House function.

"How was it?" Mom stands in the doorway, careful not to cross over the threshold.

"Good."

"It's nice to see you boys getting along," she adds.

"Mm." It is easier than lying.

Mom yawns. "Well, I should let you get some sleep."

I yawn back at her. "Good night."

She musters a limp wave and shuffles down the corridor.

I lean forward to untie my laces. Four imitation-gold statuettes stare at me. Instead of reminding me that I am the best filmmaker, director, editor and scriptwriter, they remind me of Isaac sitting in front of the camera, pitching zombie vampires, and me shooting him down. They remind me of Isaac pitching a drunken scene with Harley's endorsement. They remind me of the years

I spent as a wet blanket, walking Isaac back from the
edge while Harley tried to push him. They remind me
Harley won.

I drop the four statuettes into the bin.

Tomorrow, I start fresh.

———————

INT. COMPUTER LAB—DAY

I do not talk to Isaac at break. Instead, I work on mem-
orizing an essay for our English midterm. I move the
keyboard to one side and lay my notepad down. I take
a new page, and within ten minutes, I have a draft
paragraph. I allow myself two read-throughs. Then I tear
the page off, turn it over and attempt to reproduce it.

At Barton House, we are discouraged from learning
essays. Barton House does not produce boys who learn
by rote—that is part of the sales pitch. Then our teachers give us the grading criteria two weeks before we take
an exam, and they place so much importance on our answers to that exam that of course the best of us will use
the keywords in the criteria to build flawless paragraphs
and learn them.

My notification light flickers and I lose the sentence.
I reach for my phone.

RYAN

Come sit with us.

I place the phone back.

_____

INT. MATHEMATICS CLASSROOM—DAY

Kevin Tran leans back until the spine of his chair hits the front of my desk. "You got a pen, bro?" he asks.

I hand him my spare.

"Thanks," he says. "Catch you tomorrow."

I almost remind him that tomorrow is Saturday before I remember his seventeenth. Kevin and I are as close as two people who occasionally borrow pens off each other in Math can be, but when I agreed to go to his birthday, I had wholly expected to cancel a week or two beforehand. Isaac had rejected the invitation outright. "Who'd wanna go to a barbecue in the park with parents and no booze?" he had asked. Even though I do enjoy barbecues, do not mind parents and am a staunch believer in sobriety, I had let Isaac's lack of enthusiasm temper mine.

But I am starting fresh. "I look forward to it," I tell Kevin.

_____

INT. CORRIDOR—DAY

At lunch, I pass Isaac's locker, whose naked door is barely visible anymore. So many photographs, but none of Isaac and me.

I look to my feet and walk faster.

_____

INT. LIBRARY—DAY

I start fresh *harder*. I raid the library for every book I

can draw on in my English midterm. When I place the stack on the circulation desk, Mrs. Lang tilts her head forward a fraction.

"I would like to borrow these, please," I say.

An eyebrow climbs toward her bangs. "All of them?"

I do not flinch.

INT. COMPUTER LAB—AFTERNOON

I open the book to a page near the middle and scan it for something quotable. I do not remember the last time I actually read a book I quoted. The path to being second in the class is paved with shortcuts. Cherry-picking the sentences with intelligent-sounding words never fails to impress. Cite the author and the date of publication, and teachers will worship you.

I cherry-pick a sentence and work it into my prepared paragraph, a prepared paragraph I will not be distributing with added authenticity to anyone else. I am starting fresh.

I tear the page out, turn it over and attempt to reproduce it. Halfway through the cherry-picked quote, my mind blanks. I look up from the page and wait for it to occur to me. My eyes wander to the screen on my right.

I tear them away and clear my throat. The computer lab is my private study space. I am perfectly capable of knowing the footage is within arm's reach without being distracted by it.

I do not need to talk to Isaac. He has nothing to say to me anyway.

I blink down at the page and wait for the word. I know it sounds smart and starts with…C?

Nothing.

I surrender and turn the original paragraph over. *Coalesce.* Of course. With that block removed, the paragraph flows out of me until I hit another one. I rack my brain and my eyes drift to the computer mouse. I convince myself that the distraction is hampering my productivity.

I need to get it out of my system for the sake of the essay.

I cup my hand over the mouse and navigate my way through the shared drive folders until I come to the film folder. I double-click. The files flood in. I select ISAAC_07.

Isaac stretches his arms and yawns.

I pause him. We talk. Well, I talk, knowing full well that hearing Isaac's voice is just one click away. There is no harm in watching one clip, I suppose…

I click.

Isaac's yawn ends and his arms drop. Miles is offscreen.

MILES (O.S.)
You ready?

                    ISAAC
Born ready. Although, I have been
meaning to tell you this long-winded
story about—

                    MILES (O.S.)
No. Focus.

                    ISAAC
                    (smirking)
Do you not like my tangents?

                    MILES (O.S.)
Not when it is this late.

                    ISAAC
Aw. You know I love teasing you,
Miles.

  I smile. This is not so bad.
  I almost pause it but convince myself a little more will
not hurt.

                    ISAAC
                    (continuing)
Not sure filmmaking is your calling.
You write the best essays. Why are
you even doing this?

Isaac mirrors Miles's unseen movements, slicing his hand across his neck.

                              ISAAC
                         (continuing)
                    What does this mean?

                              MILES (O.S.)
                    Very funny.

                              ISAAC
                    I'm not going to tell people. Or am
                    I? Does that make you nervous?

My heart races. It makes me nervous *now*.

                              MILES (O.S.)
                    Please, do not even joke about it.

                              ISAAC
                         (smirking)
                    One drink and I won't tell anyone.

I close the video player.

"You rope me into selling essays," I say. "You make me
think it will bring us closer, and every chance you get,
you dangle it over me to make me do what you want.
And when I finally show up, when the wet blanket finally caves, you are high. It is never about me having
one drink. It is about me not being myself. It is about
me being Harley, being fun. Well, no. No."

I highlight all the files, right-click, Delete. A box appears to ask if I am sure I would like to permanently delete the files.

I am.

They disappear off the school server, one by one.

"No."

INT. MILES'S KITCHEN—DAY

Dad circles the table, setting the silverware. "Saw you threw out your trophies," he says. "You okay?"

"Yes. You were right—they were collecting dust."

EXT. QUEENS PARK—DAY

I walk deeper into the park, against a wave of guys marching toward the curb in muddied jerseys and the parents who follow them with folded chairs and coolers. The last of the day's scheduled games have ended, and sporting teams have relinquished the park to parties and pets.

Somewhere out there, Kevin and his family are having a barbecue. The chances of silverware are slim. I check my hands. I cannot see anything, but I can feel the bus handrails all over them.

INT. BATHROOM—DAY

I hold my hands underneath the running tap and wait for

the water to heat. It is an eternity before I feel a change in temperature, albeit slight.

A conversation carries through the brick wall. I recognize a voice. I stop the tap. It is Xavier Jones. Martin Johnson speaks too, but he is interrupted by a third person.

"No." It is short and dismissive, but it is enough for me to identify the speaker. Harley. What is he doing here? I would not think he could identify Kevin Tran from a bar of soap. Then again, from the usual look of him, I doubt he could even identify a bar of soap.

I lean into the wall until my ear almost touches the brick. I hear Omar. Harley tells them that they need to talk to Mrs. Roberts about the night Isaac died. He says she wants help.

My brow furrows. Harley is in contact with Mrs. Roberts?

They refuse to help and take Harley to task. I should relish it, but when he defends himself, his voice cracks. He almost seems…vulnerable?

They persist. He gets mad and spits out the words, "I want you to tell her he was happy."

Twigs snap under feet. He is storming off.

"When did Harley get so melodramatic?" Martin asks.

I pull back from the dividing wall. When did Harley care?

———

INT. MILES'S BEDROOM—DAY
I compose an email from the Black Ops account.

Hello, Xavier. An essay for your forthcoming English midterm exam is ready for collection. Be at Bogus Burgers at 1:45 p.m. tomorrow. Bring $50.

I send it and forward duplicates to Martin and Omar, changing their names.

I phone Isaac's home. Mr. Roberts picks up. I pinch my nose in case he recognizes my voice. "Hello, Warwick, this is Xavier."

INT. BURGER JOINT—DAY

I arrive after the lunch rush. I secure a table that has just been wiped down and take out a book. Other patrons ask if I mind moving to a smaller table. I tell them that I do mind and continue reading. When the waiter insists I order, I ask for fries and eat them slowly. I keep two fingers grease-free for turning pages.

Martin is early. He comes with a flurry of questions. I answer none. He sits opposite me. I hold out my hand and he gives me a fifty-dollar bill. I keep reading. He asks if I am going to give him his essay. I tell him we are waiting for the others.

When Xavier sees us, he punches the air and says that he knew it. "I knew you couldn't get full marks in an essay by yourself! I knew it!"

"Guilty," Martin says as Xavier eases into the seat beside him. "Pay him."

"What?" Xavier asks. "Oh." He slides the cash across the table.

I pocket it and continue reading.

Xavier cocks an eyebrow. "Well?"

"We're waiting," Martin explains.

Omar folds into the chair beside me. I turn the page and continue reading. He takes longer than Xavier to clue in. "Oh, so you guys buy essays too?"

It is a testament to how expertly we executed the operation. Martin, Xavier and Omar, who cannot go to the bathroom without texting each other in-depth updates, have kept this secret.

"What are we—?"

"Money," Martin and Xavier say.

Omar pays.

"Okay." I lean to my right. There are three personalized envelopes propped up against the front leg of my seat. I pass one to each.

"So we just learn it?" Martin asks. "How did you figure out the exam question?"

Omar has the sense to actually peer inside. "Um…" He pulls out the pages.

I try not to smirk. "What you have there are records of our correspondence and copies of the essays I have supplied you."

There is a nervous edge to Xavier's laugh. "Why?"

"You are going to have lunch with Mrs. Roberts in—" I check the time on my phone "—ten minutes, and you are going to tell her everything you remember about the night her son died, or else similar envelopes will be delivered to Mrs. Evans."

Xavier and Omar seem more worried than Martin. "But you'd be ratting yourself out," he says.

I let myself smirk. "I would be."

Martin leans back. "Shit, you're for real."

"Yes, I am." I push my chair out and stand. "You will tell her everything, and as far as she knows, you are not being blackmailed into doing it."

Omar says, "But we paid you."

"Yes, you did."

EXT. STREET—DAY

Mrs. Roberts takes large strides. I wonder if I imagine it, or if there is a sadness in the way she moves. I watch her from across the street. My view is interrupted by the occasional large vehicle stopped in traffic, but never for too long. Their discussion seems guarded; there are no big hand gestures to give me a sense of how it is going. In the end, she stands to embrace each of them in turn. They leave and instead of following, she returns to her seat.

When a worker passes, she orders fries. She empties the carton onto the tray it was served on. She eats alone.

I am not sure what I expected, but it was not this.

I helped her when Harley could not and made some money in the process. I should feel triumphant, but instead, I watch her eat with sunken shoulders. Goose bumps trace a line down from my elbow.

I take large strides of my own across the street.

———

INT. BURGER JOINT—DAY

I pass Mrs. Roberts's table, for plausibility, so I can stop, walk back, squint and ask, "Mrs. Roberts? Is that you?"

"Oh!" She covers her mouth as she chews. "Oh my." She pushes herself up.

"Fancy seeing—" An abrupt, awkward hug silences me. "This is such a small world, huh?" I point back at the counter. "I was just going to have a late lunch. Do you mind if I join you?"   .

She does not.

I order a burger that looks better than it tastes.

"I've been meaning to see you," Mrs. Roberts says. "I didn't catch you at the funeral."

"I was at the back." That is not a lie. "I liked the flowers."

"They were good flowers."

She asks about school. I tell her it is going well. She says Isaac would be proud.

It lands with more heaviness than she intends. I start counting the passing seconds in my head.

"I don't know if you believe in mediums…"

I believe in mediums and their power to prey on people who are in mourning for their own financial gain, yes.

"I went and saw one with my sister, a very talented man. Isaac spoke through him, said to tell his bright friend to keep his chin up. Not to talk badly of the others, but I think my son meant you."

I know the message is supposed to make me feel good, but it is very general and is probably repurposed to fit every deceased person somebody asks about.

"Your face..." She takes a chip. "Are you a skeptic?"

There is no use denying. "Very much so."

"Ah." She shrugs. "Well, to each their own. The way I see it, I have two choices. I can live in a world where Isaac's gone and that's it, or I can live in one where he's still here, hanging around, eager to chat. Why wouldn't I choose that?" She exhales. "*Mm*, but anyway. Let's talk about you."

"There is not really much to talk about."

"Bull." She clearly does not believe me. "Isaac would always talk about you."

I do not believe her.

INT. CAFÉ—DAY

I dip the marshmallow into the foam of the hot chocolate and take a bite. I feel heavy after seeing Mrs. Roberts, and I want to let it pass before I head home. I think about Isaac. We are all preserving our relationships with him, in our own ways. Mrs. Roberts has her medium, the guys at school have their photographs on lockers, posts on his profile, cameos in the *Herald Daily* article, and I have the footage copied to my laptop.

I cannot help but feel I have drawn the short straw.

I scroll through Isaac's article on my phone. It is less

about reading it and more about having something to do with my finger.

"Ow!"

———

BEGIN FLASHBACK:
INT. GYMNASIUM—DAY
Harley is a conscientious objector to House Competition Day. He says it promotes animosity among peers. He sits on the wooden floor of the gymnasium, leaning back on his arms. A running seventh grader steps on the sprawled fingers of his left hand.

"Ow!"

END FLASHBACK.

———

INT. CAFÉ—DAY
I look up. There Harley is, sitting a couple of tables over. He rubs his shin. He stands. I look down.

I feel him walking closer. I hope he will just walk past. He does not. He tries to make small talk. I stare at my phone. That should be enough of a hint. He sits. It was not enough of a hint.

Acting cold does not feel as good as it ought to, not after what I heard at the park yesterday. He might not be as bad as he lets on.

Before I can stop myself, I am telling him about the article. I actually share how much it hurt to be left out.

He listens. It…challenges me.

I cannot be friends with Scott Harley.

INT. MILES'S BEDROOM—DAY

I slide three fifty-dollar bills into the pouch and zip it. I push it against the back of my wardrobe and obscure it with a stack of folded T-shirts.

I lie on my bed, fully clothed, and what Mrs. Roberts said tumbles over in my mind. She has made a choice. She can live in a world where Isaac is gone, or she can live in one where he speaks to her through a medium. Surely, if Isaac really does speak through a man, that man must, when faced with a grieving mother, massage anything hurtful Isaac says so as to spare her feelings.

I have a medium of my own.

Film. It is true, an exact representation—raw, honest and unedited.

Unedited.

I roll over and scoop my computer up off the floor. I tap the edges. "Come on, come on," I coo, as if that will make it boot up faster. I try the touch pad. The cursor's response is delayed. I give it more time. When I try the touch pad again, the cursor is more cooperative, moving in time with my finger.

I open the video-editing software and import ISAAC_07 into a new project. I let it play.

Isaac stretches his arms and yawns. His arms drop. Miles is offscreen.

                    MILES (O.S.)
You ready?

                    ISAAC
Born ready. Although, I have been
meaning to tell you this long-winded
story about—

                    MILES (O.S.)
No. Focus.

                    ISAAC
        (smirking)
Do you not like my tangents?

                    MILES (O.S.)
Not when it is this late.

                    ISAAC
Aw. You know I love teasing you,
Miles. Not sure filmmaking is your
calling. You write the best essays.
Why are you even doing this?

I pause the clip and delete what comes after. I make
precise cuts and duplicate what I need. My computer
protests regularly. Video editing is beyond its specifi-
cations. It takes longer than it should, but I get it done.

I play the edit.

> ISAAC
>
> Aw. You know I love—you, Miles.
> —your—the best.—the best.

Mrs. Roberts has her medium, and I have mine. I re-play it.

> ISAAC
>
> Aw. You know I love—you, Miles.

I know it is not really him. I know footage is made of samples of the light bouncing off him, assembled to-gether to give the illusion of movement, with recorded audio running underneath. I know I have reordered those samples of light and audio recordings. But it feels so real.

> ISAAC
> (continuing)
> —your—the best.—the best.

"I love you too, Isaac," I say.

Like Mrs. Roberts, I have a choice. I can live in a world where Isaac does not like me, or I can live in one where he does. I choose the latter.

I export the new video.

I highlight all the other files in the raw-footage folder, right-click, Delete.

The last of the files disappears, and my chest feels lighter.

INT. CORRIDOR—DAY

"Hey!" Harley intercepts me on the way to homeroom. "Have you seen Thommo?" he asks. I wonder if he knows bequeathing nicknames is not mandatory.

Ryan was not in Modern History this morning.

I intend to step around Harley but he moves back into my way. He asks about my Sunday evening and I am going to be late if he keeps this up.

I cannot be friends with Scott Harley.

INT. ANCIENT HISTORY CLASSROOM—DAY

"Omar." Mr. Higgins continues to make notes on an essay he is grading. "I don't understand how you can talk all the way through my classes and still get the grades you do."

Omar peers at me from five seats over. "It's a gift, sir," he says.

"Well, gift us with your silence."

"Yeah, shut up, Omar."

The class sniggers.

Sanjay nudges me. "Harley wants you," he whispers.

Our desks snake around the room to form a U, so mine faces the corridor. I look up.

Harley is standing out there. He waves at me.

I mime, "No."

"Come on," he mouths back.

I shake my head.

He lets himself in, gets frustrated by the layout of the room and walks around the world to get in front of my desk. Mr. Higgins objects to his intrusion but Harley ignores him. He asks where Ryan lives. I write down the address. Harley hops over the opposite end of the U on the way out.

"Buffoon," Mr. Higgins mutters.

He orders us all to get back to our work.

I have no idea what that was about, but Sanjay does. He fills in Jamie. I eavesdrop. "Yeah, Rodgers texted me a couple of minutes ago," Sanjay says. "In their English class, Hughes flat out told Ms. Thomson he's gay."

"Who? Harley?" Jamie asks.

"No, Ryan."

"Ah. That's weak."

"Tell me about it. Imagine some random person telling your mom you're gay."

"I'm not gay."

"I know. I was just saying."

I interrupt their shtick for clarification. "Did you say Ryan is gay?" I ask.

Sanjay nods. "All the boarders know," he adds.

I sit back. "Huh."

Harley knows. He was in that English classroom. He should still be in that English classroom, but he charged in here to get Ryan's address. He is going home to warn Ryan.

That is almost admirable.

No. I cannot be friends with Scott Harley.

INT. MILES'S KITCHEN—NIGHT

Mom pecks the top of my head on her way around the dining table. "I don't know how you work like this."

I have spread my academic life out on the table. Books are open, stacked by relevance, and papers are scattered but ordered. Mostly. I have chopped some carrots—they are under…something.

"I have a system," I say, reaching for the middle book in a stack.

Mom fills herself a glass of water and asks how school is going.

"All right."

She keeps watching, waiting for my answer to expand to encompass Isaac.

"Better."

Mom takes a sip. "Do you miss him?" she asks.

I nod.

"How are the boys?"

Ryan is gay and Harley is admirable.

"All right," I say.

Mom accepts the answer, but I want to elaborate.

"I think I want to become Harley's friend."

Mom stifles a laugh. "That's a good thing, isn't it?"

"Harley is a Neanderthal in a private school uniform."

"You were always hard on him."

"He is more flammable than methylated spirits. He is a pharmacy with a pulse. His grammar is appalling."

Mom nods. "Yes. Valid reasons for not liking some-

one, I'll grant you that. What is it that is endearing him
to you, then?"

I think on it. "He is…nice. Or at least, I have happened to be at the right place at the right time to dis-
cover that he is occasionally not the single-worst person
in the world," I say.

Mom shrugs. "People change. People surprise us. Your
father used to be a triathlete."

"Love you, too," Dad calls from the couch.

"But look at you," Mom says, coming back over, "putting aside old differences and making new friends." She
pecks the top of my head again. "Your father and I are
proud of you, you know that?"

"Because I might befriend a Neanderthal?"

"Because of all of you," she says. She gestures at the
dining table I have commandeered. "We're very pleased."

"Well, you would want to be. I am your only one."

"That's not true," she says, circling the desk on the
way to sit with Dad. "We have a storage space in Alex-
andria where we keep all the children who have disappointed us."

———

INT. MILES'S BEDROOM—NIGHT
I message Ryan at half past nine.

ME
Are you gay?

I had workshopped other starting texts and considered building up to the question, but I figured he would appreciate directness.

He replies a minute later.

RYAN
Seriously?

All right, perhaps he does not appreciate directness.

RYAN
Haha.
Yes.

———

INT. ANCIENT HISTORY CLASSROOM—DAY
I finish my assigned work early. Mr. Higgins is busy on the other end of the U, walking a group through the task. I unzip my pencil case. My phone is inside. The notification light flickers. I angle the screen toward me and swipe to unlock it.

I have one new notification from the *Herald Daily* app. *An article you are watching has been updated.*

I downloaded the app for the sole purpose of monitoring Isaac's article.

I follow the prompts and the story loads. My eyes catch a change instantly. Isaac no longer *jumped or fell*. He only *fell*. I scan through the text, searching for an unfamiliar phrase or some new quote that contextualizes the change. Nothing. I get to the bottom and the video is gone, replaced by us.

Isaac and me. We are in the back of...

———————

BEGIN FLASHBACK:
INT. FRENCH CLASSROOM—DAY
I am assigned a seat in the back of homeroom. Mme McKenzie hovers around, making small talk, peppering sentences with *mes enfants* and *c'est bon*, I am assuming, to bewilder the students who have never been exposed to a second language. I am not bewildered. Mom and I have been working through beginner French lessons online. She is glad I have been sorted into Mme McKenzie's homeroom class. It will be useful if I carry the language through to my later years.

I turn the page and continue reading my history textbook.

The guy beside me leans back far enough that his chair touches the wall and balances on its hind legs.

"Success!" he says.

I do not react. I watch him deflate in my peripheries. He leans forward; all four legs touch the ground.

"What you doing?" he asks.

"Are."

"What?"

I hear Mom's sharp voice in my ear. *People do not like being corrected.* "Reading," I say.

"I can see that. We haven't had a class yet."

"So?"

My phone vibrates loudly on the desk we share. I panic and snatch it up.

"Busted."

Mme McKenzie is too busy exchanging basic French pleasantries with another kid whose mom discovered beginner French lessons online.

I check the message. Mom wants a photo of me in class. As subtly as I can manage, I aim the front-facing camera at myself and—

"Are you taking a selfie?" he asks.

"No."

I am. It is a new phone and I do not really know how to use it. The camera app is still open. I turn the screen away to hide the evidence.

"You *are*." He is smirking. "Who's it for? Your girlfriend?"

"I do not have a girlfriend. I am too young."

"I have a girlfriend."

I remind myself to make one up the next time someone asks.

"Who's it for, then?" he asks.

I have already torpedoed this first impression, so I say, "My mom."

"Cool."

I do not expect that. "Really?"

"No."

"Oh."

"What's she want a selfie for?"

I shrug. The less I say, the better for my social standing.

"Here." He snatches my phone, unlocks it with a swipe and angles the front-facing camera at us both.

"What are you—?"

"Doing you a favor. You want to look popular." He cleans the front of his teeth with his tongue and grins. "Smile."

"What?"

The camera-shutter sound effect is loud enough to attract Mme McKenzie's attention. Her conversation ends abruptly.

"Phone away, Isaac," she says. "You could learn a thing or two from Miles sitting next to you. Read something."

I suppress a smile as he slides the phone back to me.

"Isaac?" I ask.

He nods.

"Miles."

"I know," he says. "She told me."

"Right."

"Text it to my mom, will you?" Isaac asks. "Prove I'm making new friends."

I hesitate. "I do not have her number."

"You don't? Funny, I have your mom's. Boom."

I blink. He is waiting for a reaction.

"Right. Humor. We'll work on that," he says. "Just send the pic to me and I'll forward it. My digits are…"

END FLASHBACK.

———

INT. ANCIENT HISTORY CLASSROOM—DAY

I stare at the photograph. It is by no means perfect. Isaac

is smiling, and I am frozen midspeech. But he is smiling. With me.

It says, "We were best friends."

Isaac and I have our photo. It is everything that was good about us. We *were* best friends.

And it is in the article too. But how?

The caption reads Isaac Roberts and Miles Cooper. Image: Supplied.

Who would have supplied it?

I told only Harley. *I told only Harley.*

EXT. COURTYARD—DAY

Harley is up on the tabletop, his elbows resting on his knees and his hands limp. He sees me and becomes more rigid. Ryan is beside him. The three of us used to sit on the picnic table with Isaac. It feels like an eternity ago.

Now our diverging paths are intersecting where they started.

It feels like an ending.

I begin to cross the courtyard and fall out of myself. I picture the series finale. The shot tracks behind me. It is a full shot, one uninterrupted take. Anticipation builds, the music swells, and—

I snap back into myself.

I stop in front of them and announce, "I would like some ground rules."

"I'm great, thanks. How are you?" Harley asks.

"One. I am not the butt of anybody's jokes. Two. I am

not going to drink until it is legal for me to do so, and even then, there is no obligation. Three. I am not going to do your homework for you."

Harley shrugs. "Fine by me."

"Ditto," says Ryan.

"Oh." I had anticipated some resistance and a negotiation. "Okay."

I hop onto the tabletop and we sit in silence, the courtyard a chaotic mess around us. This is the ending. I take a deep breath, satisfied. I wait for a fade-out that does not come. Time just keeps passing.

"They're getting rid of the bench," Harley says. "Sorry, no, they're *repurposing* it. Giving it to the Industrial Tech guys to sand while they renovate this area."

"But Isaac signed it," Ryan says, peering around, "somewhere."

"Miles is sitting on it."

I lift myself up. Isaac has crudely scratched his initials into the timber. "Oh, I am."

"Another thing we lose," Ryan says. "Great."

I stare at Isaac's mark. It is an imperfection, the work of a vandal, a symptom of time. The Industrial Technology students will take the picnic table to their workshop and strip the timber back. Out of it, they will make something new. It will be better, perfect, freshly varnished, but Isaac's mark will have been erased.

"Or…" Harley looks down at the table. He assesses it through narrowed eyes. "I think the three of us could carry it," he says.

"What? We just smuggle it out?" Ryan asks.

"When everyone's in class. Or at night," Harley says. "Yeah, night's better."

Ryan considers it. "I'm game."

I want to protest, call the idea out for what it is, a reckless flight of fancy, but I can see the gears churning in their minds as they bounce ideas off each other. We will need a getaway vehicle—Harley says Isaac's sister owns a truck. We will need to enter the building after hours—Ryan can "borrow" his mom's security pass and keys. I recognize the momentum of a fresh plotline.

This is wrong. Everything is resolved. Ryan is out, Harley is not complete garbage, and I have my photo. We cannot introduce a new plotline at the end of a series finale, unless...

I have it wrong. We have established a new dynamic, and now we are plotting a caper to steal a picnic table. This is not a finale. This is the pilot of the spin-off.

Instead of a fade to black, I see our opening titles.

TITLE CARD: THE SIDEKICKS

I speak up. "You do understand there are cameras everywhere, right?" I ask.

Harley goes quiet, but Ryan is not deterred. "You said it yourself—they only look at the footage when something goes wrong."

"So?"

"So," Harley fields it, "nothing will go wrong."

———

INT. CORRIDOR—DAY

I tape the photograph to Isaac's locker, covering more of Xavier's picture than is really necessary.

We were best friends.

I step back and take in the whole collage. Various Isaacs stare at me, woven into different lives at different times. Isaac in a car, on the beach, at a formal—all smiles.

Photos are not lies. We might perform in them, but they are proof. They are evidence that two paths intersected and two people marked each other in some way, even if only for a moment. I wonder what he did for them, and they for him. I wonder if they changed each other. I wonder.

I look at Ryan's photo with Isaac. I look at Harley's. They really believe we can sneak into the school after dark and steal a picnic table. They are certain nothing will go wrong.

That is Isaac's influence. He was fearless.

I fear.

I still fear. I wonder why. I built a small empire on black-market essays—how can I still fear? Isaac had faith that I could game the system, so much that he assumed all of the risk. He reminded me I was intelligent, and that made me more so. His faith made me the sort of person who would think to pin Michael's essays on Ryan.

There is a smarter way to get the picnic table. Right now, there are too many variables. We are being foolish. I did not make all that money by being foolish.

I made all that money…

_____

INT. MRS EVANS'S OFFICE—DAY

Mrs. Evans's office looks like always—a tidy little space with the sun shouting through the window—only today, it is a monument. The last time I was in here, Isaac died.

It is funny how the past never really goes away. It sinks into the walls and whispers at you when you pass. Sitting here, I forget the time and distance between me and that moment. I picture Ryan and Harley there with me, reacting to the news.

Mrs. Evans apologizes for keeping me waiting. She turns from her computer and removes her reading glasses. Her bracelets clash together. "What can I do for you?" she asks.

"I came about the picnic tables in the courtyard. Harley says you are removing them?"

"We are, yes."

"I was wondering if I could purchase ours." I researched them online. Even an expensive picnic table would not make much of a dent in my essay earnings. "It has sentimental value."

Mrs. Evans smiles. In as delicately a way as she can manage, she tells me no.

"We used to sit there every day. Isaac even scratched his initials into it." I am willing to argue my case until she acquiesces.

Apparently, it would be unethical to accept payment from a student for a piece of school property.

"You could use the proceeds to dedicate the new fixtures to Isaac," I try.

She smiles again. "That is a very sweet idea."
But the answer is still no.

INT. MILES'S LIVING ROOM—NIGHT
We have agreed on Friday night. We will organize to
spend the night at Ryan's. Ms. Thomson will think that
we are going to see a late movie. We will be careful. If
there is the slightest risk of being caught, we leave the
picnic table and run.

I still fear.

"What are you thinking about?" Mom asks.

I unfurrow my brow and turn the page. "Nothing."

"Well, stop squinting. Why aren't you wearing your
glasses?"

"They are in my room." I turn the page even though
I have not been reading.

"By the way," Mom says, turning the cutout around
to face me. "Have you met Hector?" Her fireman bookmark is the length of her forearm.

I laugh. It would be difficult not to. "You are going
to give Dad a complex."

Mom cackles. She is at her happiest when she is play-
fully stoking Dad's insecurities. It is the best time to ask,
"Is it all right if I stay at Ryan's house on Friday?"

INT. TRAIN CAR—DAY
SUPERIMPOSE: FRIDAY

Ryan has Squad after school, so Harley and I are the ones
heading down south to pick up the car. It is the first true
test of the new regime, Harley and I alone for hours.

He puts his bag down but does not sit beside it. Instead, he starts to undress.

"What are you doing?" I ask.

The train rocks. He unzips his bag. "Getting changed.
We can't break into Barton in our uniforms," he says.

"Yes, but we can change at Isaac's?"

He stops unbuttoning his shirt. That had not occurred
to him. He shrugs and peels it off anyway.

"I'm half-done," he says.

There is a black stain all the way down the side of his
body.

"What is that?" I ask.

He looks at it. "My tat," he says.

I would not have thought it was intentional, but now
that I look closer, I can see it is a series of faded intricate
lines, melting together.

"A tree with roots," he explains.

"As opposed to a tree without?"

He scoffs and the tattoo disappears behind a black shirt.

INT. ISAAC'S KITCHEN—DAY

I emerge from the bathroom, having changed out of my
uniform. When Harley looks at me, I try not to seem
too smug, only palatably smug, because it is important
that he understand I am always right.

That said, borrowing Isobel's truck from Mrs. Roberts had been his idea, and an inspired one. There was no way Isobel would lend it to us directly, but if she thought Mrs. Roberts needed it, and Mrs. Roberts then sneakily passed it on to us, she would not be a roadblock.

Mrs. Roberts makes us tea. I enjoy it. Harley sips his with reluctance. He is drinking it only because Mrs. Roberts was the one who brewed it.

When she offers the key, I snatch it before Harley can.

EXT. SUPERMARKET PARKING LOT—DAY

Harley is out of the truck before I have even pulled the emergency brake. I shut the door and follow after him. I assume we are here for supplies, snacks and a drink that is not tea, until Harley sits on a cement curb stop in one of the free parking spots.

"Why?" I ask.

"We have some time to kill before Squad finishes," Harley says.

Not really. By the time we drive into the city, we will have twenty minutes up our sleeves, max.

"Zac and I used to chill here sometimes," he adds.

Ah. I walk over and sit beside him.

He chews on the inside of one cheek and watches the people filing in and out of the supermarket.

"Where did you find that photo of Isaac and me?" I ask. "I take it, it was you who supplied it."

"It was," he says. "Sue had it."

I picture him struggling to finish the tea. "It is good you see her."

He scrunches his nose. "It isn't really much, in the scheme of things."

"Well, no. It is not as if you blackmailed Xavier, Martin and Omar into meeting with her because you threatened to tell the school you sold them essays," I say. "No, *that* would be impressive."

"How did you even know—?"

I confess what I overheard at Kevin Tran's party and add, "Are Ryan and I your cronies now?"

"Please, stop saying that word."

I smile. This is fun, but I feel I ought to be serious, given that he has brought me to a place he used to share with Isaac. "It was good, what you did for Ryan, leaving school to tell him what happened in English."

"Damn right it was. I have detentions flying out my ass for skipping so many classes."

"And the article... I have not thanked you for it, have I?"

He is still silent.

"Thank you, Scott Harley. Like it or not, you are a good person."

"Shut up."

"You are." The compliment alone makes him squirm, so I add, "Unless I am trying to make a movie. Then you are the worst person alive."

Harley smirks. "It did need more traffic cones."

"Maybe." Not at all.

He relaxes a little. "Why don't you make another movie if you love them so much?" he asks.

Point of View was tough work, but when it all came

together in the end, it was one of the best feelings. But I had to borrow a camera from the school last year, and I would need to buy a computer that could handle the strain of video editing.

"You've got enough essay money, don't you?" he asks.

I do the sums in my head. If I lease the equipment, I probably do.

"I would need a cast," I tell him.

"Well, you know my terms."

A woman wheels a grocery cart past us toward her car. It makes Harley laugh a little.

"Zac and I used to hop in carts and take turns riding," he says.

"I am not riding around in a grocery cart."

———

EXT. SUPERMARKET PARKING LOT—DAY
SUPERIMPOSE: SEVEN MINUTES LATER
I sit in the cart. Harley pushes me. I grip the metal grille at the front and feel every bump and groove in the asphalt. The cart is only moving as fast as Harley can run, but when I close my eyes, we are speeding. I release the metal grille, one nervous hand at a time. I hold my arms out.

I am smiling.

———

INT. BURGER JOINT—NIGHT
We find Ryan in a booth near the kitchen, picking at the

only salad they have on the menu. He slams his fork down when he sees us. "There you are! What took you so long?"

We spent longer than we should have riding grocery carts; then we hit traffic; then we had to find a parking space in the city.

"Chill," Harley says. "We can't waltz in yet, there'll still be sad-sack teachers there."

I sit down and Harley says he needs to use the bathroom, only he says it with more vulgar words.

"You hungry?" Ryan asks.

"Not really." I am beginning to feel more and more nervous about what we are about to do.

"You're not wild on this, are you?"

I shake my head. I understand why we are doing it—I just wish there was another way, one that did not risk so much. I tell him so.

"You can't avoid risk. No matter what you do, it's possible something bad *can* happen," he says. "Like, I was so petrified people would find out about me. I didn't want to tell them and risk what I had." He hesitates on the edge of specifics. "I was seeing this guy. He said he could wait for me to come out, but I made him wait too long. I screwed it up. I lost that chance." He shrugs. "Who cares if we get caught? To hell with risk. Let's just do it. Life is short and I don't want to lose any more chances."

This is the first time he has opened up about liking guys. I am compelled to follow up.

"The guy… Have you told him you came out?" I ask.

"I went to his house with flowers. I wore this polo he bought me, navy blue with little white anchors on it. It was his favorite." Ryan clears his throat. "He's happy for me, but he has someone new."

Harley appears, holding two beer bottles. He slides into the booth and passes Ryan a drink.

"What are you doing?" I ask. "It is illegal for them to serve you alcohol."

"They don't need to know that," Harley whispers.

I try to look stern. "You could get fined."

Ryan and Harley clink their bottles together.

EXT. BARTON HOUSE DRIVEWAY—NIGHT

The truck pulls up to the garage entrance. My arm extends out the window. I press the security pass against the reader. The door rattles as it rises.

INT. SERVICE ELEVATOR—NIGHT

The elevator climbs slowly. My stomach churns. If a security guard spots us, we are done for. Harley leans against the back, like it is a regular Friday night for him. Ryan is enjoying this way too much. He is shifting his weight between his feet. He punches his chest to amp himself up. I blame the one beer.

"If we get arrested, is Jacs comfy with having to visit you in prison for smooches?" he asks.

"Shut up," Harley says.

"Smooches?" I ask.

"They're dating now," Ryan explains.

"Oh." I do not know how that works. When I met Jacqueline, she was flirting with Ryan. I think. Happy to leave that in the too-hard basket.

INT. CORRIDOR—NIGHT
There is something so unsettling about seeing a place you have visited only in the daytime at night. What is usually bright and bustling is dim and empty, lit only by every third overhead light.

I keep alert. My heart rages. Ryan is not helping.

When he turns the key to unlock the double doors to the courtyard, he reminds us that they may be alarmed.

"Wait, what?"

He pushes the door open.

There is no alarm. I exhale.

EXT. COURTYARD—NIGHT
We jog side by side across the yard. I picture the shot tracking behind us, one uninterrupted take. I imagine the screen splitting in half. On the other side, the security guard charges down the corridor with whatever harmful weapon guards are legally allowed to carry. My chest tightens. No. The security guard stands at a coffee vending machine in the staff room. That is better. He is watching his paper cup fill with a watery black coffee. He is not a threat.

I check over my shoulder. The building is a dark mass

against a darker sky. I search the windows for any sign
of the security guard. I do not see him, and I hope that
means he does not see us.

Harley and I grab one side of the picnic table, and
Ryan the other. He lifts highest.

"Lift!" he hisses.

"I am lifting!" I insist.

Harley sniggers. "You don't even lift, bro."

"Shut up," Ryan and I say.

We shuffle our feet across the courtyard.

Harley burps. "Sexy," he mutters to himself.

INT. CORRIDOR—NIGHT

We move slowly. Circles of white travel from one edge
of the tabletop to the other as we pass under each light.
It feels like progress. Slow progress.

"Isaac would love this," Ryan whispers.

He would. I search for his carved initials the next time
we pass under a light. I do not see them. I wait for the
next light and check again. Nothing.

"Wait, wait," I whisper.

"What?"

"Drop the table."

We drop the table. I run my fingers across it.

"This is not ours," I tell them.

The others search for the scratched initials. We cannot find them.

"Shit," Harley mumbles. He burps again.

We haul the table back. My steps are short and panicked. We are making reverse progress.

EXT. COURTYARD—NIGHT
We leave the picnic table by the doors and sprint over. We run our fingers across the tabletops, squinting in the dark, searching for our table. We cannot find it.

Ryan's phone goes off. The ringtone echoes in the empty courtyard.

"Shit."

"Are you kidding?" I ask. "You left your phone on?"

He takes it out and swears again. He angles the screen toward us and my heart sinks. *Mom* is flashing.

"Why is she calling?" Ryan asks. "She thinks we're in a movie."

"Answer it," Harley says.

"Do not answer it," I warn.

Light floods the courtyard.

INT. MRS EVANS'S OFFICE—NIGHT
As the deputy headmistress of Barton House, Mrs. Evans deals with two types of students: delinquents and athletic achievers. She looks at us severely.

Tonight we are the delinquents. She yawns into her hand and lists our offenses, which include stealing a teacher's security pass and keys, trespassing after hours and attempting to steal school property.

Ms. Thomson reported her lost items on Friday afternoon. Had she not, Mrs. Evans explains, using her pass to enter school so late would have registered as an abnormal activity and notified security. We were caught before we had even entered the parking garage.

Mrs. Evans sighs. "I should expel you."

I expect her to say she "will" expel us. "Should" is weird.

EXT. RYAN'S HOUSE—NIGHT

The motion sensors out front detect the truck pulling into the driveway. The garden lights come on, illuminating a picnic table in the middle of the lawn.

Mrs. Evans organized to have it delivered after I asked her to sell it to me.

I knew there was a smarter way.

The three of us stare at it, mostly in disbelief.

"Fancy a test-drive?" Harley asks.

We climb onto the tabletop. I almost sit on Isaac's initials. I move to the right of them. Ryan sits tall, chest broad. Harley sinks back onto his elbows.

I sigh, satisfied. I like this series.

I imagine its story arc. Ms. Thomson comes out here in the next few minutes to give us an earful. One Sunday, Ryan mans the barbecue, burns the lamb chops but serves them on this table anyway. On what would have been Isaac's eighteenth birthday, we drive the picnic table to his parents' place. Harley brings a case of beer and we toast him. They drink; I pour my bottle into the garden when no one else is looking. On Isaac's twenty-sixth, we move the table to Ryan's rooftop. He has moved in with a guy from his swim team. They lean into each other. They laugh. Harley reaches for a beer and Jacqueline slaps his wrist. She touches her growing midsection. If she cannot drink, neither can he. They have a boy. They call him Zac. Ryan has his own, two girls. We still have barbecues on Sundays. They become monthly. When the kids start school, it is harder to get time off work. We text. We message on Isaac's thirty-second. We imagine what he would have been like. We forget his forty-ninth. By then, the picnic table is in my garage, underneath two decades of boxes. We wonder if it was always this hard to move. We sit on top and before the night is done, we carve our initials beside his.

I snap back into the present. I cannot wait to watch that series, even if it does not turn out exactly as I imagine.

We sit still. The garden sensor does not detect movement. The light switches off and we fade to black.